There was no crowd for him to get lost in, just a few people scattered here and there, and so the seven men behind him had no fear of losing him. They fanned out and walked briskly with their eyes burning into the back of the thief's head, while the song built in suspense, the trumpet coming in on his headphones to stir up his blood and turn his adrenaline from fear to excitement.

When the sax began to wail, his stride became a bit cockier and he turned for the black wrought-iron railing and the open sky beyond it. The men pursuing him looked at one another in confusion. Was he deliberately going to box himself in? No. It couldn't be. As one, they realized he was going to jump for it.

They picked up the pace, and he saw them in the mirrors on the frames of his sunglasses.

He had to risk them getting a little closer if he was to time his escape just right, and he knew it was stupid, but since there weren't too many opportunities to do this, he might as well do it with style. He waited a few more seconds for just the right part of the song before digging out the lanyard of his bungee cord and making a mad dash across the boardwalk.

They bolted after him and the song neared its crescendo as he threw the lanyard, snapping it onto a park bench that had been bolted into to the ground. He stepped up onto the bench without breaking stride and sprang onto the railing, launching himself out into the open air, spinning around with one hand touching his lips and blowing them a dramatic kiss.

Also by the Author

the Prince of Foxes

For Quinn,
It was a pleasure
to meet you, and I hope
you enjoy the book!
Alexander Ferrar

Alexander Ferrar

This is a work of fiction. All of the characters portrayed in this book are fictitious, and any resemblance to real people or events would be ridiculous. Really. Should any resemblance seem apparent between characters or events in this book and you or your own life, you surely live in a world of make-believe. Seriously, it's preposterous.

THE PRINCE OF FOXES

Copyright © 2015 by Alexander Ferrar

ISBN: 1511748281

Published by Heretics Abroad, a division of 3MTC
First edition: May 2015

Cover art and illustrations by Alexander Ferrar

A Note on the Text

The text of this book was set in Hoosegow Linotype, a font created by the renegade typesetters known as the Black Hand, as a way of protesting the evil committed by the Church against Gutenberg. Note the sharp angularity and arrogant curlicues that characterize their style. Interesting bit of trivia: the Black Hand were the ones responsible for the practice of making S's look like F's in early prints, such as "Ye Olde Blackfmith" and "Officef of the Magiftratef of the Ftate of Maffechuffettf," as a way of knowing who in a crowd of strangers was sympathetic to their cause and weeding out the ignorant. A member of the clandestine cognoscenti would, while reading, smile to himself and say nothing, whilst an enemy of the cause would say "By Jove, what nonfenfe is thif?!"

www.alexferrar.com

This is dedicated to Aidan, Madeline, Ethan, Calvin & Drew

I

In a beautiful antique bronze egg-and-dart frame with its wire resting on the latest top-of-the-line security sensor, on a wall in the most prestigious museum of art in Zenda, the capital of Ruritania, Bart Simpson was pulling his pants down and shouting "Eat my shorts!" Approaching footsteps of echoing loafers on the cold marble floor were getting louder in the distance.

"I can't wait to see it," one man's voice said.

"It's amazing," said another. "I must have stared at it for a good twenty minutes when it was unpacked, and for well over an hour once it was hanging on the wall."

"Is it really that good?" a third asked.

"Oh, yes. You have no idea."

A fourth voice asked, with more than a trace of sarcasm: "Did it give you Stendhal's?"

"You know," said the second voice. "I can't say whether it did. I don't know if such a thing exists, like that article says, but I can say my breath was taken away. I may not have been catatonic from the sheer beauty of the painting, but I had no wish to look away from it." The voices got steadily louder.

"I must say I'm curious," said the first voice. "I mean, a Japanese woman breastfeeding *a leopard cub?* And it somehow doesn't look tacky?"

"Oh, there's nothing tacky about it at all. When you see it and can tell that the woman was merely defending herself out in the wild from its mother, and did what she had to do to protect herself, and then saw the cub and felt sorry for leaving it an orphan, there is such beauty in the selflessness of her act that you will want to go out and do charitable acts yourself."

"Pardon my skept—" began the third voice, and there was a scuffing of loafers on the marble as they halted before the frame, and four sharp intakes of breath.

Bart's canary-yellow face and bared buttocks, and his navy blue shorts and panic-button red shirt hit them in the face like a bucket of cold water.

There was a moment of stunned silence before the man of the first voice could stutter "It's…it's *gone!*"

"Thank you, Charles," said the fourth man, coldly, as he remembered himself and unclipped his CB radio from his belt, bringing it to his lips and barking "Security!"

The other two men found their voices and whispered their shock. What could have happened? Who could have *done* this? Why, they felt absolutely raped! This must be a joke.

A terrible, terrible joke.

They had the finest security system in the world!

It was top-of-the-line! It was unbeatable!

The first voice stammered "Who…who on Earth could *do* such a thing?"

At that moment, the man who could do such a thing was strutting down the sidewalk with the painting "Bodhi-sattva" in a tube hanging from a strap over his shoulder. From his headphones plugged into the smartphone in his pocket, the Beastie Boys were shouting the glories of dis-tilled spirits, firearms, and solace found in the arms of fallen women, when the ringtone interrupted at the most touching part, and he dug it out with a grin. Looking at the display, he grinned wider and answered.

"Halloo?" His bushy mustache was starting to peel off.

There was still a bop in his step as he walked, as if the music had not stopped.

"Yep. Got it and am on my way to the train station."

He sidestepped an elderly gentleman, nodding to him, and smiled at a young couple holding hands.

"Mm-hmmm." He smoothed his mustache back on.

He passed a sign on a bus stop's side panel that made him do a double-take. He paused, looking at it, reading the name Lex Cargo and looking at the photo of a swarthy man standing with bare feet spread wide, holding a fluffy white cat. Between his feet was a small wooden box with a tiny dog standing on it and looking up at him and the cat, poised as if ready to try and jump. The man had that fashion models' look of contemptuous eyes and slightly parted lips, as if he had found himself breathless while being arrogant.

The corner of the man on the phone's mouth twitched in a brief smile, and he kept walking.

"Uh-huh?" he said. "Why do I not like the sound of that? 'As long as you're in Zenda…?' It sounds like you're about to say something I really don't want to hear. Just like that time in Egypt when—no, no, I'm not arguing, I'm just saying—"

He stopped, and the young woman who was walking right behind him was brought up short, and glared at the back of his head before moving to walk around him.

"No, it was a joke. And no, Egypt was really no trouble at all. Aside from almost getting killed twice. Joke, joke," he added, even though it wasn't a joke.

He started walking again. "Right, so go on. As long as I'm in Zenda…?"

He listened a moment, then stopped abruptly once more.

"Are you sure that's necessary?"

The man walking behind him bumped into him, glared at his back, and moved around to walk on.

"I am *on my way* to the train station. Another few steps and I'm home free. Security is going to be all over this place in a few minutes and I'm one step ahead of them."

He sighed, his shoulders sagging.

"No. No, it's no problem at all."

He listened a moment and his head fell forward to hang in defeat, his eyes scrunched tight and his teeth bared.

He nodded.

"Sure. Sure, I can do it. I'll just be arriving a little later."

He waited, nodded again, and said good-bye, hanging up. Took a deep breath, raising his face to look at the sky.

Stared at the clouds for a long moment, at the satellite well beyond the blue vault of the sky that bounced the encrypted signal of his cell phone all over the planet.

Let his breath out slowly and said "Sssshoot."

About two hours later, he strolled as casually as he could out of a tall gray building that reached to the sky and beyond.

In his pocket was a USB that now contained an important double-secret-confidential file, and he could not walk away as quickly as he wanted to for fear of arousing suspicion, but he knew every calm and measured step he took let the black-clad security goons get closer and closer to him. He'd just crossed the street diagonally when the mirror-glass doors of the building swung open, spilling out seven men in black behind him. The one in the lead, a sandy-haired man with crow's feet on an otherwise young face, pointed at the thief hurrying away toward a nearby boardwalk.

The thief put on a pair of sunglasses with mirrors on the sides of the frames so he could watch the men behind him. He got to the corner as they were crossing the street. One of them, a dark-haired one, talked into his cuff with a fist held up to his face. The thief put his headphones back in and chose a song on his phone, 'King's March' by Glenn Miller. The song began with low, ominous notes, befitting the occasion, and he gauged the distance from the corner to the bridge up ahead to see exactly where he would have to break into a run.

There was no crowd for him to get lost in, just a few people scattered here and there, and so the seven men behind him had no fear of losing him. They fanned out and walked briskly with their eyes burning into the back of the thief's head, while the song built in suspense, the trumpet coming in to stir up his blood and turn his adrenaline from fear into excitement.

When the sax began to wail, his stride became a bit cockier and he turned for the black wrought-iron railing and the open sky beyond it. The men pursuing him looked at one another in confusion. Was he deliberately going to box himself in? No. It couldn't be. As one, they realized he was going to jump for it.

They picked up the pace, and he saw them in the mirrors.

He had to risk them getting a little closer if he was to time his escape just right, and he knew it was stupid, but since there weren't too many opportunities to do this, he might as well do it with style. He waited a few more seconds for just the right part of the song before digging out the lanyard of his bungee cord and making a mad dash across the boardwalk.

They bolted after him and the song neared its crescendo as he threw the lanyard, snapping it onto a park bench that had been bolted into to the ground. He stepped up onto the bench without breaking stride and sprang onto the railing, launching himself out into the open air, spinning around with one hand touching his lips and blowing them a dramatic kiss as the song hit its swaggering climax.

Enraged, the men in black spurred forward, pulling small stun guns from holsters beneath their jackets, hoping to shoot him while he was still in range.

The headphones managed to stay stuffed in his ears, but in the rushing wind as he plummeted to the grass far below, his false mustache slipped off of his upper lip and fluttered away.

The sandy-haired man saw it and wondered for a moment what it was, but was too busy trying to shoot the falling man.

One of the others looked at the length of bungee cord that was about to start stretching and snapped open a little wicked-looking knife with a two-inch blade and started sawing away at it, right where it attached the lanyard. Another saw what he was doing and thought it would be easier to just unhook the lanyard, and they both got in each other's way long enough for the bungee cord to stretch as far as it would go.

At that split second that any longer and he would be rocketed back up and into stun gun range, the thief cut his end of the bungee cord and fell the rest of the way to the ground, the black rope snapping elastically back up at the men in black.

They flinched and backed up a step, and he hit the grass in a shoulder roll that saved him from a broken back.

The sandy-haired man glared down at him and there was a moment that they both froze in time as he looked back up and met those baleful eyes. The thief swallowed, then realized he was being seen without his false mustache, so when he turned to hurry away, he pulled off his navy blue sweater and let them all see the great big false tattoo he had on his left arm.

The sandy-haired man blinked, like the shutter of a camera clicking.

II

Guy Fox was not Futuro Quackenbush's real name.

He had hated his real name so much that he changed it on his eighteenth birthday down at the local courthouse, and told everyone except his parents by noon that day. They'd've been more than a little disappointed in him, his parents.

The reason for naming him Futuro had sprung from their stoner days when they'd watch cartoons in the afternoon, and there had been a girl dressed in all white armor who had come from the future—where they all apparently dressed that way—and she fought crime or something and her name was Futura.

What're the odds, they thought, that someone should find a way to travel back in time, know how to fight, be of the disposition to fight crime, and just happen to be named Futura of all things? Really, what were the odds? Like, how many people in the future would name their daughter Futura, for starters, and of aaaaall the people on the planet at that time, *she'd* be the one to go back in time? Not Jennifer so-and-so. Or Wendy.

So, since the present is the future for everybody that ever lived up until now, they should go ahead and name their child Futuro and train him to be the savior of someone else that he would just happen to stumble upon when he'd inevitably fall down the rabbit hole. Martial arts, sword fighting, all sciences that could be confused with magic if practiced in the presence of primitive people, and all manner of escape artistry.

It came as a bit of a surprise, and as quite a bit of a disappointment, that he never did actually fall into a rabbit hole, or invent a means of time travel, or fulfill any kind of a prophecy whatsoever. He merely grew up a very clever, resourceful, fit, and rather dangerous young man.

With a chip on his shoulder about his stupid name.

He'd had to explain his name to everyone at the beginning of every class, every year at school, and to every friend he had made between, and some people made fun of him, and he had shown them his significant prowess in kung fu and ninjutsu at a very early age. That won him fame on the playground, and at the beginning of his teenage years, considerable appeal with all the girls. He also knew how to dance, speak several languages, and build things that impressed adult engineers.

He won a scholarship to an Ivy League school, and there was spotted by a CIA recruiter, one of the many who watched from the shadows for any "sons of privilege" who exhibited the signs they were looking for. He was discreetly approached, brought into covert service, and amazed everyone at Camp Peary—the "Farm"—from the very start. He would be the future of espionage.

The Farm is where he learned how to pick locks, wear disguises, enter secured buildings, cross borders illegally, use invisible ink, survive torture, parachute jump, create small explosives, and elude surveillance. He was wise enough not to share too many of his own secrets, like how to breathe underwater. He learned much and shared little

His second greatest accomplishment was the invention of a cloaking device that astounded his peers and superiors. He'd come up with it as the result of a late-night debate over sci-fi movies. Someone had said that invisibility was impossible, and therefore stupid, and someone else had said that that was the point of science fiction. It was stuff that couldn't happen. But then someone else pointed out that a lot of that stuff certainly *could* happen because it *has* happened. Space travel. Ansibles. If it can be dreamt, it can be built.

That first someone then posed the question to Guy and all the others within earshot turned expectantly for his ruling. He sat back in his chair and tapped his lips with his index finger a moment, then nodded.

"Yes. We can make someone invisible. But it's going to be expensive."

A suit was made with hundreds of tiny cameras that would film whatever was happening all around him, and show those images on hundreds of screens on the opposite side. From any angle, anyone looking at him saw the image of what was behind him, and it wasn't perfect, but it was pretty damn close.

That was his second greatest accomplishment.

His first was the one that got him fired.

Back safely in his hotel room, Guy took off his clothes to strip off the cloaking suit he'd had on beneath it, the one he'd used to infiltrate two high security buildings in one day. If it'd not run out of batteries in the middle of his escape, he'd be able to put it back on when the authorities eventually closed in on him, and stand there in the same room as them, but since it had *so* many cameras and screens to power, it only worked for a short time and took forever to recharge.

He went to the window and parted the drapes slightly with his fingertips to gaze out on the city beneath him. A thousand lights were coming on in the gathering dusk.

Somewhere out there, many people were looking for him, and he should've been long gone. The security detail from the art museum, probably the police, and definitely the vengeful men in black from the second job, the absolutely unnecessary copying of a file from the offices of Count Rupert of Hentzau.

Eluding the police was a piece of cake, if you managed to stay one step ahead of them. Security from the museum might be a bit tougher, unrestricted as they were by protocol. But Hentzau was well-known for the great lengths he'd go to protect his privacy. It was said that he employed the Dreadnaughts, the group of twelve ruthless mercenaries that had overthrown five dictators and despots in as many years, to do his dirty work.

Guy didn't need that kind of a headache, but hey, what's done is done.

The ringtone of his phone sounded and he let the drapery fall back into place, turning back to where it rang on the bed-spread. He snatched it and sprawled onto the queen-sized bed, bouncing a little to arrange himself and get comfortable, saw it was his wife, and answered with an indulgent smile.

"Why, hallo Meester Bond," he said.

"Hello, Mr. Bond," she said. They both always called each other Mr. Bond. Long story. "Where are you?"

"I am safely ensconced."

"Do you have everything?"

"I do indeed. I'll be out of here first thing in the morning. God willing," he added—his way of saying 'Knock on wood.'

"Good. Then high-tail back here into my loving arms."

"Roger that. So whatchoo doing?"

"Mmmm," she said, and he knew she was stretching like a cat and smiling that smile that bewitched him. "Missing you." He kept the conversation pleasant, not mentioning that he was angry about being in his current situation, because it wouldn't make things any better.

They talked for almost an hour, the way people talk when they're in love, which is tedious to everyone but them. Inevitably, a fight started about why he wasn't coming back as scheduled, and he had to hear about what he probably did wrong, what he should have done instead, and all the things that could happen to him if apprehended. In the end each one waited for the other to hang up first, and when it was finally silent in the hotel room, Guy turned on the TV.

There was nothing yet on the local news about him, so he started flipping the channels. Commercial, commercial…

He saw thirty seconds' worth of some stupid movie about a guy whose parents were down on him for being a layabout and not doing anything with his life, and he rolled his eyes. He already knew it would be the same movie they made ten times every year—the kid refused to grow up and, in the end, his very childishness was what saved the day, proving that the parents didn't know what they were talking about. It encouraged the kids in Audienceland who watched it to go on being idiots.

He changed the channels and saw either reality shows that encouraged people to cause public scenes, or news about what event was attended by which celebrities and what they wore.

"Who was there? What did they wear? Why should I care?" he muttered.

He turned the TV off and stared at the black screen for a long moment. Slowly, he began to nod his head to a tune only he could hear, and slowly, the lyrics to that tune came out in a low chant: "Don't go down to the bar, don't go down to the bar, don't go down to the bar."

He swung his legs over the side of the bed and sat up for a moment, struggling against his will.

"Don't go down to the bar, don't go down to the bar,"

and he stood up and went to his suitcase. "Don't go down to the bar." Now he was doing a little dance as he sang, looking for something to wear. "Don't go down to the bar."

He put on cream slacks and black moccasins with a red and blue ribbon that went with his navy blue fencing sweater. It had a gold crest with rampant lions on the right breast and a wide white chevron inverted across the chest. A shield flanked by golden olive branches was under his left trap with words in gold beneath it: "The harder the struggle, the greater the glory." Two crossed foils on each shoulder announced that this was the zip-up sweater of the Williams Fencing Club.

All the while advising himself not to go down to the bar.

He checked himself in the mirror, smoothed his hair and popped his sweater's collar, then turned sharply on his heel to march to the door, saying "Do *not* have more than one drink, do *not* have more than one drink..."

He strode with a hint of swagger down the green-carpeted hall to the gold doors of the elevator, and waited there, bouncing on the balls of his feet to the tune he was humming.

"Do *not* have more than one drink, do *not* have more than one drink..."

When he entered the bar he quickly sized up everyone that he could see. No one was a potential threat, and one of them in particular piqued his interest. He went to lean against the bar in front of the man toweling off wet glasses and said in a French accent *"Monseur, s'il vou* plaît—"but the bartender said "Sorry, Mack. English or German."

"*Pardón.* A good scotch if you please."

"*Avec plaisir.*"

Guy made an effort not to roll his eyes, and watched the reflection of the man he had seen in the mirror behind the bar. He was sitting alone at a table in the corner in a shiny purple shirt he'd unbuttoned down to his navel, a brown fedora with a spotted feather sticking out of the band, some Jackie Onassis sunglasses, and a scarf. He looked like he was making a big show of being inconspicuous.

"Who's he?" Guy asked the bartender quietly.

The man glanced at the corner. "Lex Cargo."

"Really? What's he doing, hiding out?"

"Yep. He's gone underground."

"Not doing a very good job of it."

"Your Scotch, sir."

"*Danke,* Fritz."

Guy took his drink over to the table in the corner, right up to the man sitting there and offered his hand.

"Lex Cargo?"

The man looked astonished, and was about to deny he was the famous artist when Guy held up a reassuring hand.

"It's okay, your secret is safe with me. I just wanted to tell you that I'm a big fan."

Cargo relaxed.

"Thank you," he said, in a Guatemalan accent. "I guess my disguise wasn't that great, huh?"

"Well, with a face like that how could you expect not to be recognized? Especially when your new show is about to open?"

"*A la gran!* That's why I am in hiding," he said despondently, squirming in his seat.

"Why? Because you don't want to be seen before—?"

"No! Because there is an international crime syndicate out to ruin me!"

Pause.

"Um…really?"

"Yes! They've already broken into the museum where

the show is to be and *stolen* one of my paintings!"

Gasp.

"Stolen?" Guy asked, pulling up a chair and sitting.

"Indeed! This very day!"

"But how is that possible? That art museum is said to have the finest security system in the world!" He knew that he shouldn't have, but he couldn't help himself.

"They said as much, but unless it was an inside job—which it most assuredly was not—then it could only be the work of a clandestine crime organization, like that of Moriarty, or Keyser Sozé. Oh, and I just *know* they'll come after me next!"

"But…but what if they don't? What if they only wanted the painting?"

"Ha ha! My naïve friend, no one could ever be satisfied with just one. Once the sickness is upon them, they have to have it all, and they will stop at nothing until they get it!"

Guy cut his eyes off to the side and pursed his lips.

"Erm…not necessarily."

"Oh no, trust me on this. I have done extensive research."

"Have you now?"

"I have."

"In that case, what if this alleged 'theft' which cannot be perpetrated by anyone except either Moriarty, or Keyser Sozé, or must be an inside job by one of, if not *the* most reputable establishment in the Western World, is just a publicity stunt?"

"Hmm? What do you mean?"

"What if the museum is just pretending to have lost it?"

"Of what benefit could that be to them?"

"The free publicity for the show and for you created by all the buzz out on the street."

"They would be made to look like fools."

"Maybe not."

"Hmmm. I don't know. Maybe."

"Well, let's have a toast, then, shall we? To the winds of Fate."

"And how whimsical they can be. Chin chin!"

They clinked glasses and drank.

"So," Guy asked when they had swallowed and grimaced. "Which painting is missing?"

Lex made a face. "Bodhissatva. It's not one of my best but it really *means* something, and that's what bothers me most."

"What do you mean?"

"I mean…technically it is not beautiful, and it is annoying that so many people don't get it right away, and dislike it because they think it's something sexual, perverted, so they need it to be explained to them and *then* they like it. I feel I should not have to explain it. But since I do, in that I have failed."

"People think it's sexual?"

"Some. I've had people try to interpret it as a metaphor of the violence in sexuality."

"The what?"

"I know. A girl from Berkeley said it."

"Is there violence in sexuality that I'm unaware of?"

"Apparently. I guess I'm not doing it right either. Anyhow, any who!" He finished his glass and signaled the bartender.

"So what's going on about the painting?" Guy asked. "The authorities are out in full-force, I imagine."

"I dunno. I'm a little nervous, that's why I'm here, keeping a low profile, yunno? I just have a feeling Moriarty's boys are going to snatch me up and ransom me for all the money they think I have, and cut off my fingers one by one and mail them to my mother when I tell them I'm just not as rich as everybody thinks."

"But…" Guy said. "I've been following your career. Your work sells for millions of dollars."

"I don't get those millions," Lex said ruefully.

"What? Why not?"

Lex made a show of biting his tongue, and Guy knew he wasn't going to leave after just one drink any more. He also turned and signaled to the bartender.

One of the men sitting at the bar was watching their conversation in the bisected mirror behind the bar. He had heard one of the men say "millions" but didn't quite hear the reply. As he strained to listen, he noticed the one who was speaking more quietly now. He knew he'd seen him somewhere before.

"Oy," he said to the bartender. "Who's that bloke there?"

"That's Lex Cargo, the famous artist."

"He don't look like a famous artist."

"He's in disguise."

"Really?"

"Yeah. He normally has a necklace on."

"Ohhhhh."

The man had another sip of his drink and pulled out his phone, calling someone and stepping off his stool to get some privacy. The bartender paid him no attention.

III

Guy Fox had learned many of the deep, dark secrets of the United States during his stint in the CIA, and one of them was that the bogus Abstract Art scandal was a cover-up for money laundering, making large amounts of money disappear whenever they needed to fund a coup in some other country. When arms were needed by someplace like Guatemala or Iraq, that's when people like Jackson Pollock, Robert Motherwell, Willem de Kooning and Mark Rothko came into play.

The story they allowed to be told was a semi-patriotic one. In the Cold War, the CIA promoted Abstract Expressionism, supposedly as propaganda against the Soviets, as proof of the creativity and intellectual freedom of the West. In the late 1940s, the dominant art movement in Russia was that of realistic paintings, showing the appeal of stoicism and discipline, a bit of a justification for communism. Allen Dulles, who headed the CIA, couldn't stand it. There had to be something so fundamentally different that could catch on quickly and put the Soviets back into the shadows where they belonged.

It is well-known among those who control the masses that if something is going to catch on in the US it has to have what they call a low-ability threshold. It must be something that any monkey can do easily, like hula hoops and Tamagotchis. When the opportunity to be a part of something new and trendy is as easy as pie, everybody will jump on the bandwagon. So, telling the world that going to all the trouble of painting something realistic is passé, everyone who wants to be called an artist—while putting forth minimal effort—will jump at the chance.

What was funny is that many of those artists were, in

fact, ex-communists and certainly not likely to receive backing from the government in the McCarthy era. They had little respect for the government and none whatsoever for the CIA. That was what the CIA thought would make it work. No one would *ever* suspect them. The connection was improbable at best.

The Propaganda Assets Inventory had in its heyday more than eight hundred newspapers and magazines and other news sources to play whatever tune the CIA wanted the world to dance to that week.

Then there was the International Organizations Division, under Tom Braden, that funded and promoted jazz musicians, books and films that made the Soviets look bad, like George Orwell's *Animal Farm*, and bad art that even the President said was trash. Many years later, Braden would say: "We wanted to unite all the people who were writers, who were musicians, who were artists, to demonstrate that the West and the United States was devoted to freedom of expression and to intellectual achievement without any rigid barriers as to what you must write, and what you must say, and what you must do, and what you must paint, which was what was going on in the Soviet Union. I think it was the most important division that the agency had, and I think that it played an enormous role in the Cold War."

So, millionaires like Nelson Rockefeller were asked to say that they liked Abstract Expressionism, and support it publicly. Paintings of senseless scribble or simple fields of flat colors began to sell for millions of dollars. The low-ability threshold of art was at its lowest point since prehistoric cave drawings.

As a consequence, just like children who play in Little League in the US stop trying so hard to win when they see they'll all get a trophy anyway, and even come to expect a trophy for everything they do in life afterwards, the quality of art plummeted. Any monkey could do it, and the new avant-garde now held in contempt anyone who held true to any real discipline, tarring them with the same brush as the cold, rigid Soviets.

As one raised from birth to be a champion, Guy detested the ever-more-common belief that one could get by with minimal effort. And now he found himself in a conversation with the only famous artist in the world who seemed to be dragging the art world back to where he felt it belonged.

And he'd just stolen his painting earlier that day.

"So, after the gallery takes their commission, and after the taxes, and this that and the other thing that I don't really understand, I end up with a pretty small amount of money."

Guy nodded, sympathizing, feeling like a jerk and knowing that the real reason Lex wasn't getting paid as much as everyone thought was that those funds were really going to supply weapons to Syria.

And feeling like a jerk for taking the painting.

He had just never come face to face with the artist before, had always considered the victim of his thefts to be some big corporation or a museum that could handle the loss. Plus, he felt a bit of guilt too for the way the CIA had waged their unjust, illegal, and devastating secret war against Guatemala back in the 1950s. He had nothing to do with it, but since he'd been with the Agency he still felt responsible.

"Man, that stinks," he said, not knowing what else to say. But at least it was something.

"Well, here's to that stinking," Lex announced, lifting his glass for another toast. *Clink!*

They drank and talked and drank and talked for hours, and they didn't notice more men coming in to join the man at the bar who kept watching them in the bisected mirror.

At one point, Guy was ready to confess what he had done and hand the painting back over to Lex, and had ordered one more drink to steel himself. It was a tough decision to make, and more scotch would make it easier to face all the problems that would follow. But before he could drink, Lex asked him his name, and in his guilt-driven honesty, Guy told him.

"Guy? You mean like, just, Dude?" Lex asked, laughing.

"No, it was a name long before people started calling men guys. In fact, it was because of a certain man that guys are now called guys. Guy Fawkes."

"Where have I heard that name before?"

"Remember, remember, the Fifth of November."

"Mmmm, nope."

"Okay, back when Catholics were being treated like dirt in England, this rebel named Guy Fawkes tried to blow up the House of Lords. He got caught, and people've been celebrating the day of his capture by wearing masks that look like him. You know that group called Anonymous? Those masks they all wear? Those are Guy Fawkes masks. Anyway, on the nights that they wore the masks and set off fireworks and lit bonfires the men were being called 'guys' and at some point, it stuck."

"Oh. I'd never thought of that."

"Well, I take a bit of an interest in the origins of things."

"Really? Like what else?"

"Like ordinary everyday things we do. Like say 'Bless you' when someone sneezes."

"Oh, that's because your heart stops for an instant."

"No, it isn't."

"Yes, it is. That's what my sister said."

"Oh. Is your sister a doctor?"

"No, but she knows all kinds of things."

"Well, I'm afraid she doesn't know that. It's because Pope Gregory the Great was being overwhelmed by people petitioning him to bless their relatives when they started sneezing. The early symptom of the Plague was sneezing. But he couldn't go around blessing all of Europe, especially for the common cold or a simple Oh-it's-chilly little sneeze, so he said God told him that in this case it was okay for people to have the authority to bless one another."

"Ha! Really?"

"Yep."

"Cool. What else?"

"Well, this may be relevant to you as a Spanish speaker." Lex Cargo sat up.

"Do you know the story of the Castilian lisp?"

"Oh yes! King Ferdinand spoke with a lisp and everyone adopted a lisp of their own to be polite, so that he would not feel self-conscious about it."

"That's a good story, but it's just that. A story."

"Como?"

"The one who had a lisp was Pedro I, almost two hundred years before the dialect evolved, and it is no more a lisp than saying 'thimble'. It is just a different pronunciation. In the US, people will pronounce the same word differently everywhere. What my uncle calls the rubber around a car's wheel sounds to me like that sticky black stuff on the beach. That's not from a speech impediment. It's just the way people talk in different places. In the US lots of people say the countries they are at war with are 'Eye-rack' and 'Eye-ran' instead of "Ee-rock' and 'Ee-ron.' Or the country they will be at war with soon is 'Paky-stan' instead of 'Pock-ee-stahn'."

"So, why the lisp in Barthelona, then?"

"It's just, Barcelona was a Greek colony. There is more of a tendency to pronounce words like that in Greece. That's all."

"Oh. That's not as good."

"I know, the Ferdinand story is a better story but man, the Spanish don't like to hear people tell it."

"Anyhow, any who. What about you? What do you do?"

"Ha ha! You sound like a Dr. Seuss book!"

"Do I? I didn't mean to."

"It was funny."

"Sorry."

"That's okay. Me? What do I do? Well, I'm between jobs."

"Meaning?"

"Meaning I do this and that, but my career, as it were, ended a few years ago, before it even got started."

As he was a bit drunk, Guy wasn't being as secretive as he normally was, as if he had to get something off his chest.

"Oh dear. And your career was?"

"Well, I worked for a short time with the CIA."

There. I said it.

"You're joking."

"Nope."

"Really?"

"Scout's honor. But I quit. Or rather, I was fired. Or more like it was a bit of both. I chose to get fired."

"Because you didn't like what you were doing?"

"That's part of it. I was so disillusioned with the role that the Agency had played in world politics. I had been led to believe that they were the good guys trying to make the world a better place, and that was *not* the case at all. Finding out about the Agency raising money to stage coups in other countries by selling crack didn't help."

"What?"

"Well, indirectly. They sent tons of cocaine to Danilo Blandon in San Francisco, who sent it down to 'Freeway' Rick Ross in South Central LA, who made it into crack. That's what started the crack epidemic in the US. Basically, the Agency poisoned the people they were supposed to protect so they could afford to trick other people into killing each other. Plus the Guatemala, United Fruit thing."

Lex briefly closed his eyes and lifted a hand in a gesture that meant 'Yeah, that.' Guy went on.

"But, I had a very bright future there, and I was putting my morals on the back burner, so to speak. They said I was going to be the future of espionage, that I was going to change the world.

"And then she walked into the room," he added quietly.

Lex waited while Guy watched some memory resurfacing. The change that came over the thief's face as he gazed off into nothing was like warm light.

"We had big plans," Guy said. "All my friends and fellow spies. And we were in a restaurant in Langley, Virginia, talking excitedly about what we were going to do, using code words so the people sitting around us wouldn't understand. We had finished dinner and were having drinks and were talking and laughing and being proud of who we were, like the kids at the party before they go off to war. Yunno, "On this, St. Crispin's Day!" and all that. A merry band of brothers. And then, all of that, all of my fine castles in the air just melted away because a girl walked in."

Lex sat up in his chair again. "Tell me."

"I hear that ringing to this very day, the big jingle bells that they'd hung from the door that would announce to the staff that someone had walked in. I heard them and glanced over to see the most beautiful girl in the world walk in."

Lex smiled. "I love stories like this."

"I was transfixed. I mean, she lit up the whole room just walking in. My friends all stopped laughing when they saw my face and turned to see who it was I was looking at, and yunno how you can feel someone watching you? Feel their eyes burning into you and you turn and see them? They can be watching you from a crowd, but you'll turn and look directly into their eyes? Well, I watched her feel the burn of my eyes and catch me looking at her." He smiled bashfully, remembering being caught. "And she just smiled at us. She smiled that smile of someone who knows she's hot and doesn't resent it when men are stunned by her beauty. Didn't roll her eyes or anything like a lot of girls do, like they are insulted by the compliment."

"I wouldn't know," Lex said with a smirk.

"Well, she didn't. She just smiled and walked on, looking around for the people she was supposed to meet."

"And what did you do?"

"Well, I let the guys make fun of me for a while, and they all went back to whatever we'd been talking about that just wasn't important for me anymore. Saving the world from this terrorist or that crisis just faded away, and I knew from that moment that the only thing that mattered was her."

"Wow. What did she look like?"

"An exquisite face. Apricot skin, smoky almond eyes, wine red Cupid's-bow lips. Long black hair in a French braid down to the small of her back…"

"So, what did you do?"

"Ha! It was funny. Well, no, it's funny now, but at the time I was dead serious. I started thinking about what I would have to do to get that girl. Save her from drowning, save her from a fire, save her from the white slavers who'd come to grab her in the night. As it turns out, the best thing to do was wait until I saw her again and go up to her and say Hello."

"Really? No pick-up line? No contrived situation?"

"Nope. Just an honest Hello."

"Wow. And what's the lucky lady's name?"

Guy smiled the smile of the cat that got the canary.

"Mrs. Fox."

Finally, the bartender flicked on the lights to tell everyone it was time to split. There were groans of protest, but he made a What-can-I-do? face and shrugged. Tabs were paid and hugs given by people parting ways, good-byes were spoken and luck wished. Five evil men at the bar seemed to stiffen in readiness.

Lex stretched and yawned like a leopard in the shade, and Guy thought again about giving him the painting, but changed his mind and decided to break into his room and leave it there while the artist slept. He just had to see which room was his.

He had been sitting with one leg crossed, the ankle resting on his other knee, and he twisted the heel of his shoe to reveal several tiny gadgets set in sunken niches matching their shape. He wedged a finger into one of the niches to pop out a small round silver thing, something that looked like a watch battery. Using his knee to slide the heel back into place, he peeled off a plastic sticker that kept the adhesive clean on one side, and he palmed the tiny GPS tracker.

When Lex stood up, Guy rose with him, and when the artist offered his hand to shake, Guy surprised him with a warm hug instead. The GPS tracker slid deftly up under the collar of Lex's shiny purple shirt and stuck there.

"Well," Lex said. "I wish you the best in everything you

do and I must say that Mrs. Fox is very lucky lady."

"Thank you. I wish you the best of luck with your opening and I am sure you will get your painting back."

"Ugh!" Lex rolled his eyes theatrically, backing away. "My fingers are crossed. Good night, *amiguito!*"

Guy watched him leave, and thought 'What a nice fellow.' Then he felt the burn of eyes upon him and glanced at a man at the bar who looked sharply away. It was a burly man in a long black leather coat, with stubble on his strong meaty jaw the same length as the close-cropped hair on his head. He had looked away so quickly that it was obvious he'd been watching intently, and Guy was instantly on guard. The other four men standing with Stubble were birds of his feather, and they were all watching Lex walk out the door.

Guy pulled out his smartphone and pretended to scroll through Facebook so the thugs wouldn't know he was already on to them. Quickly, he turned on the camera and tried to take as many surreptitious photos of them as he could, but they all came out blurry. He had to stop when Stubble glanced back at him and almost saw what he was doing. He turned and walked off to the Gent's, making sure they saw him go.

"Ee wos takin' ah pitcha," Stubble said to the others. "I'm show of it."

"We'll see bout that," said another, leaving to follow Guy.

"Maybe you should go wittim, Trevah," Stubble said. "He looks a bit fit. Might tax ol' Danny Boy wot wiff 'is bum leg."

The one called Trevor sized Guy up and nodded.

"He'd give Daniel a run fo' 'is money, he would. We'll be along in a jiffy. Ah think the three of ya 'ave that poof in the bag and doan need us two."

"Roight."

Trevor followed Danny following Guy into the bath-room, leaving the other three to follow Lex down the green-carpeted hall to the golden doors of the elevator, grabbing him halfway down and wrestling him sideways through a service entrance.

IV

When Danny pushed open the Men's room door, Guy was nowhere to be seen, so the thug was instantly suspicious. His quarry was most likely hidden in a stall, crouched on the seat of a toilet and waiting to pounce on him, so he must already know that they already knew that he knew that they knew that he was on to their game. He paused, carefully looking behind the door to make sure Guy wasn't waiting to hit him from behind, because that's exactly what he would have done, and when he saw that no one was there, he proceeded cautiously.

Letting the door shut quietly behind him.

Passing right underneath Guy, who waited, like a spider above the door in the corner where the wall met the ceiling.

Guy's knees and elbows were shaking from the strain of pushing so hard to keep himself there, and it was a great relief to let go when the door was closed beneath him and out of his way. He pushed off hard with his legs as he dropped, and his prey turned just in time to see him and gasp as he crashed into him. They hit the cold tiles hard, the thug cushioning the fall a bit, but the impact still jarring Guy enough to stun him.

Just in time for Trevor to walk in.

Cursing, the newcomer sprang into action, tackling Guy.

Rolling him over and sitting down hard on his chest so he couldn't block his punches or hit back, Trevor grabbed Guy's face to turn it and get a better target for his knuckles. In the movies, the hero always manages to rock his legs up and kick the bad guy in the back of his head, but Trevor knew that was physically impossible, so he wasn't worried. It was Hollywood.

Guy also knew that was impossible, so he didn't bother

to try. Instead, he made a big fist out of both of his pinned hands and pressed it under Trevor's tailbone before he had a chance to strike. There is a cluster of nerves there that made the thug jump a little, giving Guy just enough room to twist and put his shoulder up, keeping Trevor a few inches above him for the split second he needed to slip out from under him.

Trevor, outraged, swung blindly behind him and managed to hit Guy in the side of the head, and Guy lost his balance on the tiles. By now Danny was struggling to get up. He'd slipped a disk in his spine, and was uncomfortable, but not out of commission yet. Trevor scrambled to his feet and turned to aim a kick at Guy's face.

Steeling himself, Guy rolled himself quickly toward Trevor who, surprised, hesitated. While Guy could not possibly gather enough momentum to bowl Trevor over, like in the movies, it still startled him and made him stagger a bit, off-balance as he was from the kick he had yet to deliver.

Much closer now, Guy reached around and swung, hitting the back of Trevor's knee from behind. It wasn't hard enough to knock him down, but still made him shiver reflexively and stagger more. Guy wrapped one arm around Trevor's leg and grabbed it with his other hand, squeezed, and his would-be assailant went down hard, crashing right on top of Danny.

Guy got to his feet, still holding Trevor's leg wrapped in his arms, but he loosened his grip enough to back up a bit, to let his grip slide from the shin to the ankle, and there he made his grip tight again and leaned back, making Trevor scream.

Letting go, he stepped in and kicked Danny full in the face as he tried to rise, full in the baleful glare of his hard grey eyes.

He knew he should take that chance to make his getaway. Every second he stayed outside of his hotel room was one more chance to get caught, and held long enough for police to arrive and put together that he was the culprit in two thefts. If he had any chance to get away, he couldn't dilly-dally.

He couldn't resist, though. These two had to be marked, if only to make them recognizable to the authorities later.

Swiveling on his heel, Guy swung his arm and dropped to put all of his momentum into a punch that blackened both of Trevor's eyes. The force cracked the thug's head back into the cold tiles and knocked him out. Rolling to his feet, Guy turned on Danny and battered him black and blue with savage blows that could be heard from behind the bar.

The bartender and the few remaining customers had all been staring at the Men's room door, with open mouths, since they'd heard Trevor's scream, and now watched the blond wood with stricken eyes, frozen by the shock of it.

A long moment passed, and then the door swung open, the man the bartender would incorrectly remember later as being French coming out. The door closed slowly behind him, obscuring the brief view they'd all had of two badly beaten men on the floor.

They stared at his face, which he wrinkled up in anger at his stupidity in coming out that night, in taking a risk, and now being in danger because of it. They watched him all the way to the exit, and then were distracted by the horrible smell coming out of the Men's room, a smell that made them gasp.

One of Guy's inventions that had gotten him noticed by the CIA recruiting officer back in University had been a new method of tracking down criminals. For some time, banks have had decoy stacks of money in the tellers' drawers with dye packs in them, little bombs of bright red dye that would explode all over a bank robber after he left the building.

The idea was that a bright red man is easier to find fleeing the scene of a crime. Guy thought, however, that a bright red man can still hide behind a tree, or in some bushes, or catch a ride from someone driving by.

A lonely woman or a confused young man might pull over to help a bright red fellow who'd just robbed a bank because it would offer adventure and excitement to spice up their lives.

If that dye pack was full of skunk spray, however, nobody in the world would let them get in their car. No cop would roll right past a tree with his quarry hiding behind it, and if he tried to get lost in a crowd, that crowd would part like the Red Sea and leave him a sitting duck for the pursuing officers.

Guy's skunk pack won him instant notoriety on campus, a small fortune in selling the idea to security companies, and the attention of the CIA recruiter.

Now, a smaller version of it, taken from the sliding heel of his other shoe, was making the two thugs in the Men's easier for the authorities to find. Everyone they passed when they staggered to their hideout would remark on their stench and remember it, and probably gossip about it, and be happy to tell the police what the men looked like when they follow up on the anonymous tip Guy planned to give later on.

He was sure those goons had come to do some kind of harm to Lex, and they probably had him in their clutches in a dank cell somewhere. He was now glad he'd placed a GPS on him earlier. He would be able to locate the hideout if the police could not track down the two stinky men, but he *really* didn't want to get involved, since he had not only the police looking for him, but the henchmen of the dreaded Count Rupert of Hentzau.

It's just, he liked the artist. Lex was a nice guy. And he was responsible for him being in this situation. So, he had to find and rescue him. And that would take time.

Speaking of the dreaded Count Rupert of Hentzau, at that very moment his private jet was touching down at the Zenda International Airport—a long black jet with an especially dastardly-looking crimson H emblazoned on it.

Without waiting for the seatbelt light to go off or the tone to go *ding!* twelve evil men rose ominously from their seats.

The one in the first seat moved with the sinuous grace of a panther. His head was shaven except for a long, braided black scalp lock, and there was cruelty in the thin lips framed by his Fu Manchu mustache. He, like the eleven Dreadnaughts that followed him, was heavily tattooed and wore many weapons in discreet hiding places all over his body, from knives and ninja throwing stars to pistols that sprang with a *snick!* out of their sleeves, into ready hands.

They were the demons that Hentzau kept on a leash, and he was Zaporavo, their captain. It was said that he could track a bird on a cloudy day, and he'd been trained by blind monks in a temple carved out of the living rock of an active volcano, in a jungle where even monsters feared to tread. In martial arts there was no equal in all the world, because no one who'd ever challenged him had survived.

The flight attendant, a pretty French woman named Odile, smiled pleasantly at him as he passed, and said *"Bon nuit"* to all of the others, one after the other, until they were out of the jet and, hopefully, out of her life forever. She crossed herself and rolled her eyes, letting out a heavy sigh. *"Mon dieu!"*

A small man in a brown suit awaited them, pushing up his glasses and trying to decide how to stand. He kept holding his left wrist with the other hand in front of him, then doing the same with his hands behind him, then putting his hands in his pockets and jingling his keys, then unbuttoning his jacket and putting his hands on his hips, then buttoning it back up and starting all over again.

When they finally arrived in the terminal, he knew better than to offer his hand. Zaporavo would never deign to shake it.

"Mr. Zaporavo," the man said. "I trust you had a pleasant flight." He turned and started walking quickly to keep up with the mercenary, annoyed with himself that he had to. "The dear Count would like you to visit his building at once and see how the burglar got in, what he may have taken, and find him soon as you can. We will need him alive, of course, and coherent."

Zaporavo said nothing. There was murder in his eyes.

V

Count Rupert of Hentzau was one of the evilest men in the world, and the patriarch of the—undisputedly—most evil family in the world. The Borgias would have learnt a lot from them. It would perhaps be beneficial to recount the history of the dreaded Hentzau family, in order to give one a better understanding of just how evil they were, and what a grave error Guy Fox had made earlier that day.

The Hentzaus have been in control of the world, pretty much all of it, for a long time, with their tentacles reaching into many aspects of our daily lives, and they obtained this position through lies, manipulation and murder.

It happened thus:

In 1743, a man named Mayer Amschel Bauer was born in Frankfurt, Germany, the son of a money lender and the proprietor of a counting house. His father, Moses, placed a red sign above the door to his counting house, a red hexagram which, under Hentzau instruction would end up on the Israeli flag two hundred years later.

As an adult, Mayer Amschel Bauer worked for a bank in Hanover, owned by the Oppenheimers, where he was very successful, and he became a junior partner. Whilst there, he became acquainted with General von Estorff.

When his father died, Bauer returned to Frankfurt to take over the family business. Seeing a significance in the red hexagram, he decided to change his name from Bauer to Hentzau, which means "Red Shield." As Mayer Amschel Hentzau, he discovered that General von Estorff had become attached to the court of Prince William IX of Hesse-Hanau, one of the richest royal houses in Europe. They'd gained their wealth by the hiring out of Hessian soldiers to other countries for various wars.

He remade the General's acquaintance and was introduced to the Prince himself, with whom he began doing business. He found that loaning money to governments and royalty is more profitable than loaning to individuals, as the loans are bigger and are secured by the nation's taxes.

Hentzau began planning a secret organization in 1770 with a friend, Adam Weishaupt, outwardly a Roman Catholic, that would be based upon the teachings of the Talmud.

They called it the "Illuminati" or "keepers of the light."

Three years later, his first son, Amschel, was born. Like all of his brothers, he would enter the family business at twelve. Solomon was born a year later, and Nathan one after that.

Adam Weishaupt finished his organization of the Illuminati on May 1, 1776. The purpose of the group was not to oppose the Catholic Church, as legend tries to convince us, but to divide all Gentiles through political, economic, social, and religious means. They'd be supplied with weapons and given reasons to fight amongst themselves until they eventually destroy one another, leaving the "meek" to inherit the Earth.

Weishaupt managed to infiltrate the Continental Order of Freemasons with his Illuminati doctrine and established lodges of the Grand Orient to be their secret headquarters. Weishaupt also hired two thousand of the most intelligent men in Europe to 1) Use monetary and carnal bribery to obtain control of men already in high places, in various levels of all governments and business. Once influential people had fallen for the temptations of the Illuminati they were held in bondage by blackmail, threats of financial ruin, public exposure and fiscal harm, even death.

2) The faculties of universities were to cultivate the better students from families of privilege, and recommend

them for special training in internationalism, or the idea that only a one-world government could end recurring wars and strife. That training was sponsored by the Illuminati.

3) All influential people controlled by the Illuminati, either by deceit or by training, were to be used as agents and placed behind the scenes of all governments as experts and specialists, so they could advise the top executives to adopt policies which would in the long-run serve the secret plans of the Illuminati one-world conspiracy and bring about the destruction of the governments and religions they were appointed to serve.

4) Obtain absolute control of the press, and slant all news and information in order to make the masses believe that a one-world government is the only solution to our many and varied problems.

In 1777, Nathan Mayer Hentzau was born.

In 1784, Adam Weishaupt issued his order for the French Revolution to be "started" by Maximilien Robespierre, with a book written by one of Weishaupt's associates, Xavier Zwack, and sent by courier from Frankfurt to Paris. However, *en route,* the courier was struck by lightning, of all things. The book detailing this plan was discovered by the police, and handed over to the Bavarian authorities. As a consequence, Bavarian police raided Weishaupt's masonic lodges of the Grand Orient, and the homes of his most influential associates. The Bavarian authorities saw that the book was a very real threat, and outlawed the Illuminati and closed all Bavarian lodges of the Grand Orient.

The next year, Mayer Amschel Hentzau moved his family into a five-storey house in Frankfurt, which they shared with the Schiff family, and the year after that, the Bavarian government published the details of the Illuminati plot in a document entitled *Original Writings of the Order and Sect of the*

Illuminati. They then sent this document to all the heads of church and state throughout Europe, but sadly their warning was ignored.

In 1788 Kalman Mayer Hentzau was born. Due to the European ignorance of the Bavarian government's warning, the Illuminati's plan for a French Revolution succeeded the following year. This revolution was a banker's dream, as it established a new constitution and passed laws forbidding the Church from levying tithes, and removed its exemption from taxation. Mayer Amschel Hentzau is quoted as saying "Let me issue and control a nation's money and I care not who writes the laws."

A warning was hidden in the Bible about "the Beast," or Satan on Earth, traveling among us. His sign is 666, a reference in code to the hexagram symbol of that evil family. Sadly, the reference was taken literally and people think it warns of a red guy with horns and a goatee, and aren't taken seriously. In Revelations 13, it says "And he causes all, the small and the great, and the rich and the poor, and the free men and the slaves, to be given a mark on their right hand or on their forehead, and he provides that no one will be able to buy or to sell, except the one who has the mark, either the name of the beast or the number of his name. Here is wisdom. Let him who has understanding calculate the number of the beast, for the number is that of a man; and his number is six hundred and sixty-six."

It is not a prophecy of something that a diabolical super being will someday commit to bring the people of the world under his thumb. It is a warning of the plan the Hentzaus have of controlling the world. They are realizing this dream with the RFID chip, which they hope will be implanted in people's hands and will eventually store all their information so that, if anyone ever opposes them, they can simply turn off that person's chip. The power to render someone, with the press of a button, completely powerless, would make them gods.

In 1791, the Hentzaus gained control of another nation's money through Alexander Hamilton, their agent in George Washington's cabinet, when they set up a central bank in the US called the First Bank of the United States, established with a twenty-year charter. The next year, James Hentzau was born.

In 1798, John Robison published a book entitled *Proofs of a Conspiracy Against All the Religions and Governments of Europe Carried on in the Secret Meetings of Freemasons, Illuminati and Reading Societies.* In this book, Professor Robison of the University of Edinburgh, one of the leading intellects of his time, who in 1783 was elected general secretary of the Royal Society of Edinburgh, gave details of the whole Hentzau Illuminati plot.

He wrote about how he'd been a high degree mason in the Scottish Rite of Freemasonry, and had been invited by Adam Weishaupt to Europe, where he was given a revised copy of the conspiracy. He pretended to go along with it, to get as much information as he could, and then published his exposé, including details of the Bavarian government's investigation into the Illuminati and the French Revolution.

That same year, on July 19th, David Pappen, President of Harvard University, lectured the graduating class on the influence Illuminism was having on American politics and religion.

At the age of 21, Nathan Mayer Hentzau left Frankfurt for England, where with a large sum of money given to him by his father, he set up a banking house in London.

In 1806, Napoleon stated that it was his "object to remove the house of Hess-Cassel from rulership and to strike it out of the list of powers." Upon hearing this, Prince William IX of Hesse-Hanau fled Germany, went to Denmark, and entrusted his fortune—valued at three million dollars at that time—to Mayer Amschel Hentzau for safekeeping.

Nathan Hentzau wed Hannah Barent Cohen, the daughter of a wealthy London merchant, and their first son, Lionel, was born two years later. Two years after that, Sir Francis Baring and Abraham Goldsmid died, leaving Nathan as the remaining major banker in England. Solomon Mayer Hentzau then went to Vienna and set up the bank M. von Hentzau und Söhne. If this were a movie, ominous music would start playing.

The charter for the Hentzaus' Bank in the US ran out in 1811 and Congress voted against its renewal. Nathan Mayer Hentzau was not amused and he said "Either the application for renewal of the charter is granted, or the United States will find itself involved in a most disastrous war." Congress stood firm and the Charter wasn't renewed, so Nathan told the British to "Teach those impudent Americans a lesson. Bring them back to colonial status." Backed by Hentzau money, and Nathan's orders, the British declared war on the United States. The plan was to cause the US to build up such a debt in the War of 1812 that they'd have to surrender to Hentzau and allow the charter for the First Bank of the United States to be renewed.

Mayer Amschel Hentzau died, and in his will laid out specific laws that the House of Hentzau were to follow: all key positions in the family business were only to be held by family members; only male members of the family were allowed to participate in the family business, this included a reported sixth secret bastard son (It is important to note that Mayer Amschel Hentzau also had five daughters, so today the spread of the Hentzau Zionist dynasty without the Hentzau name is far and wide, and Jews consider the mixed offspring of a Jewish mother is solely Jewish); the family was to intermarry with its first and second cousins to preserve the family fortune (of the eighteen marriages by Mayer Amschel Hentzau's grandchildren, sixteen were between first cousins); no public inventory of his estate was to be published; no legal action was to be taken with regard to the value of the inheritance; and the eldest son of the eldest son was to become the head of the family (this condition could only be overturned when the majority of the family agreed otherwise). Nathan Mayer Hentzau was elected head of the family.

Jacob Mayer Hentzau went to Paris to start the bank de Hentzau Frères. There's that music again. Then Nathaniel de Hentzau, the son-in-law of Jacob Hentzau, was born.

Now, remember the $3,000,000 Prince William IX of Hesse-Hanau had entrusted to Mayer Amschel Hentzau for safekeeping? An account of what happened next can be found in the Jewish Encyclopaedia, 1905 edition, Volume 10, page 494, which indicates the money was never returned by Hentzau to Prince William IX of Hesse-Hanau. It also says that "Nathan Mayer Hentzau invested this $3,000,000 in gold from the East India Company, knowing that it would be needed for Wellington's peninsula campaign."

On the stolen money Nathan made,

"no less than four profits:

i) On the sale of Wellington's paper which he bought at 50 cents on the dollar and collected at par;

ii) on the sale of gold to Wellington;

iii) on its repurchase; and

iv) on forwarding it to Portugal."

In 1815, the five Hentzau brothers supplied gold to both Wellington's army, through Nathan in England, and to

Napoleon's army through Jacob in France, and began their policy of funding both sides in wars. The Hentzaus loved wars because they are massive generators of risk free debt. This is because they are guaranteed by the government of a country and therefore the efforts of the population of that country, so it doesn't matter if that country loses the war because the loans are given on the guarantee that the victor will honor the debts of the vanquished.

Whilst the Hentzaus were funding both sides in that war, they used the banks they had spread out across Europe to set up an unrivalled postal network of secret routes and fast couriers. The post carried was to be opened up by these couriers and their details given to the Hentzaus so they always were one step ahead of current events.

Furthermore, these Hentzau couriers were the only merchants allowed to pass through the English and French blockades. They kept Nathan Hentzau up to date with how the war was going so he could use that intelligence to buy and sell from his position on the stock exchange.

One of Hentzau's couriers was a man named Rothworth. When the Battle of Waterloo was won by the British, Rothworth took off for the Channel and was able to deliver this news to Nathan Mayer Hentzau, a full twenty-four hours before Wellington's own courier. At that time British bonds were called consuls and they were traded on the floor of the stock exchange. Nathan Mayer Hentzau instructed all his workers on the floor to start selling consuls. That made all the other traders believe that the British had lost the war, so they started selling frantically.

The consuls plummeted in value, and then Nathan Mayer Hentzau discreetly instructed his workers to purchase all the consuls they could lay their hands on.

When news came through that the British had actually

won the war, the consuls went up to a level even higher than before the war ended, leaving Nathan Mayer Hentzau with a return of approximately twenty to one on his investment. This gave the Hentzau family complete control of the British economy, now the financial center of the world following Napoleon's defeat, and forced England to set up a new Bank of England, which Nathan Mayer Hentzau controlled.

Interestingly, a hundred years later the New York Times ran a story reporting that Nathan Mayer Hentzau's grandson had attempted to secure a court order to suppress publication of a book with this insider trading story. He claimed the story was untrue and libelous, but the court denied the request and ordered the family to pay all court costs. Maybe because in 1815, Nathan Mayer Hentzau made his famous statement, "I care not what puppet is placed upon the throne of England to rule the Empire on which the sun never sets. The man who controls Britain's money supply controls the British Empire, and I control the British money supply." He would go onto brag that in the seventeen years he had been in England he had increased the £20,000 stake given to him by his father, 2,500 times to £50 million.

The Hentzaus also used their control of the Bank of England to replace the method of shipping gold from one country to another, instead using their banks spread across Europe to set up a system of paper debits and credits, the banking system of today. By the end of that century, a period known as the "Age of the Hentzaus," it is estimated that the Hentzau family controlled half the wealth of the world.

However, something that did not go well for them that year was the Congress of Vienna, which started in September, 1814 and concluded the following June. The Congress of Vienna was for the Hentzaus to create a form of world government, to give them complete political control over much of the civilized world. Many of the European governments were in debt to the Hentzaus, so they had that as a bargaining tool. However, Tsar Alexander I of Russia, who had not succumbed to a Hentzau central bank, would not go along with it, so the Hentzau world government plan failed. Enraged, Nathan swore that, some day, he or his descendants would murder Tsar Alexander I's entire family. He was true to his word—one hundred two years later, Hentzau-funded Bolsheviks would carry out that promise.

In 1816, the American Congress passed a bill permitting yet another Hentzau-dominated central bank, which gave the Hentzaus control of the American money supply again. This is called the Second Bank of the United States and was given a twenty-year charter. The British war against the US ended with the deaths of thousands of British and American soldiers, but the Hentzaus got their bank. That was the price of saying No.

VI

Following the French securing massive loans in 1817 in order to help rebuild after their disastrous defeat at Waterloo, Hentzau agents in 1818 bought vast amounts of French government bonds, causing their value to increase. On November 5th they dumped all of them on the open market, causing their value to plummet and France to go into a financial panic. The Hentzaus then stepped in to take control of the French money supply. This was the same year the Hentzaus were able to loan £5,000,000 to the Prussian government.

In 1821, Kalman Mayer Hentzau was sent to Naples, Italy. He would end up doing a lot of business with the Vatican, and Pope Gregory XVI subsequently conferred upon him the Order of St. George. Whenever the Pope received Kalman, he would give him his hand rather than the customary toe to kiss, which showed the extent of Kalman's power over the Vatican.

In 1822, the Emperor of Austria gave the five Hentzau brothers the title of Barons.

The next year, the Hentzaus took over the financial operations of the Catholic Church, worldwide. The money of Jesus was officially in the hands of the Beast.

In 1827, Sir Walter Scott published his nine-volume set, *the Life of Napoleon,* and in Volume Two he stated that the French Revolution was planned by the Illuminati and financed by the money changers of Europe.

In 1832, President Andrew Jackson, the seventh President of the United States from 1829 to 1837, ran the campaign for his second term in office under the slogan, "Jackson And No Bank!" in reference to his plan to take control of the American money system to benefit the American people, and not for the profiteering of the Hentzaus.

In 1833, he started removing the government's deposits from the Second Bank of the United States and instead deposited them into banks directed by democratic bankers.

This caused the Hentzaus to panic and do what they do best, contract the money supply, causing a depression.

President Jackson knew what they were up to and later said "You are a den of vipers and thieves. I intend to rout you out, and by the Eternal God, I will rout you out."

In 1834, an Italian revolutionary leader, Giuseppe Mazzini, was selected by the Illuminati to direct the revolutionary program throughout the world, and would serve in that capacity until he died in 1872.

On January 30, 1835, an assassin tried to shoot President Jackson, but miraculously, both of his pistols misfired. They were found to work perfectly. President Jackson would later claim that he knew the Hentzaus were responsible. The would-be assassin Richard Lawrence was found not guilty by reason of insanity, and bragged that powerful people in Europe had hired him and promised to protect him if he were caught. The story has since been changed in the history books, which now say that President Jackson blamed the Whig Party. In fact, the history books have been changed quite a bit.

In 1836, following his years of fighting the Hentzaus and their central bank in America, President Andrew Jackson finally succeeded in throwing the central bank out of the US, when the bank's charter was not renewed. It would not be until 1913 that the Hentzaus could set up the third central bank, the Federal Reserve, and to ensure no mistakes are made, this time they would put one of their own bloodline, Jacob Schiff, in charge of the project.

When Nathan Mayer Hentzau died and the control of

his bank, N. M. Hentzau & Sons passed on to his younger brother, James Mayer Hentzau, they sent one of their own, August Belmont, to America to salvage their banking interests defeated by President Jackson.

In 1840, the Hentzaus became the Bank of England's bullion brokers. They set up agencies in California and Australia.

The next year, President John Tyler—the 10th President, from 1841 to 1845—vetoed the act to renew the charter for the Bank of the United States. He received hundreds of letters threatening him with assassination.

Benjamin Disraeli—who would go on to become British Prime Minister twice—published *Coningsby,* in which he called Nathan Mayer Hentzau "the Lord and Master of the money markets of the world, and of course virtually Lord and Master of everything else. He literally held the revenues of Southern Italy in pawn, and Monarchs and Ministers of all countries courted his advice and were guided by his suggestions."

A year later, the Great American Patriot, Andrew Jackson died. Before his death, when asked what he regarded his greatest achievement, he said without hesitation "I killed the bank."

Jacob Hentzau, who by then had married his own niece, Betty, Solomon Hentzau's daughter, and was known as Baron James de Hentzau, won the contract to build the first major railway line across the country. It was called the Chemin De Fer Du Nord and ran initially from Paris to Valenciennes and then joined with the Austrian rail network built by his brother—and wife's father—Solomon Mayer Hentzau.

In 1847, Lionel De Hentzau, now married to his cousin, the daughter of his uncle, Kalman Mayer Hentzau, was elected to the parliamentary seat for the City of London.

A requirement for entering Parliament was to take an oath as a Christian. Lionel De Hentzau refused to do this, as he was Jewish, and his seat in Parliament remained empty for eleven years until new oaths were allowed. He must have been an invaluable representative for his constituency, bearing in mind he could never vote on any bill as he never entered Parliament. It is a mystery how he managed to keep his seat for eleven years without ever showing up to sit in it.

In 1848, Karl Marx published *the Communist Manifesto.* Interestingly, at the same time as he was working on this, Karl Ritter of Frankfurt University was writing the antithesis which would form the basis for Friedrich Wilhelm Nietzsche's *Nietzscheanism*, which was later developed into Fascism and then Nazism, and used to foment the First and Second World Wars.

Marx, Ritter, and Nietzsche were all funded and under the instruction of the Hentzaus. The idea was that those who direct the overall conspiracy could use the differences in those two so-called ideologies to divide larger factions of the human race into opposing camps, so they could be armed and brainwashed into fighting and destroying each other. Particularly, to destroy all political and religious institutions.

Before her death in 1849, Mayer Amschel Hentzau's wife, Gutle Schnaper, said nonchalantly that "If my sons did not want wars, there would be none."

In the 1850s, construction began on the manor houses of Mentmore in England and Ferrières in France, and later, more Hentzau Manors would follow throughout the world, all of them filled with works of art.

Jacob Hentzau in France was said to be worth 600 million francs, which at the time was 150 million francs more than all the other bankers in France put together.

In 1852, N.M. Hentzau & Sons began refining gold and silver for the Royal Mint and the Bank of England, and other international customers. The next year, Nathaniel de Hentzau, son in law of Jacob Hentzau, bought the Château Brane Mouton, the Bordeaux vineyard of Mouton, and renamed it Château Mouton Hentzau.

In 1855, Amschel, Solomon, and Kalman died, the last of the nicer Hentzaus. There was nothing but trouble after that.

Three years later, Lionel De Hentzau finally took his seat in Parliament when the requirement to take an oath was made to include other oaths. He became the first Jewish member of the British parliament.

In 1861, President Abraham Lincoln—the 16th President of the United States from 1860 until his assassination by the Hentzaus in 1865—approached the big banks in New York to obtain loans to support the ongoing American Civil War. As these large banks were under the influence of the Hentzaus, they offered him a deal they knew he could never accept: 24% to 36% interest on all monies loaned.

Lincoln was so angry that he printed his own money and informed the public that this was now legal tender for all debts public and private. By April of 1862, $449,338,902 worth of Lincoln's money had been printed and distributed.

He said, "We gave the people of this republic the greatest blessing they ever had, their own paper money to pay their own debts."

That same year, the Times of London ran a story saying that "If that mischievous financial policy, which had its origin in the North American Republic, should become indurated down to a fixture, then that government will furnish its own money without cost. It will pay off debts and be without a debt. It will have all the money necessary to carry on its commerce. It will become prosperous beyond precedent in the history of civilized governments of the world. The brains and the wealth of all countries will go to North America. That government must be destroyed or it will destroy every monarchy on the globe."

Otto von Bismarck, the Chancellor of Germany, said later: "The division of the United States into two federations of equal force was decided long before the civil war by the high financial power of Europe. These bankers were afraid that the United States, if they remained in one block and as one nation, would attain economical and financial independence, which would upset their financial domination over the world. The voice of Hentzau predominated. They foresaw the tremendous booty if they could substitute two feeble democracies, indebted to the financiers, to the vigorous Republic, confident and self-providing. Therefore they started their emissaries in order to exploit the question of slavery and thus dig an abyss between the two parts of the Republic."

In 1863, President Lincoln discovered the Tsar of Russia, Alexander II, was having problems with the Hentzaus as well, for refusing their continual attempts to set up a central bank in Russia. The Tsar then gave Lincoln some unexpected help. He ordered that if either England or France actively intervened in the American Civil War, and helped the South, Russia would consider such action a declaration of war, and take the side of President Lincoln. To show he wasn't making empty promises, he sent part of his Pacific Fleet to port in San Francisco and another part to New York.

The Hentzaus' banking house in Naples, Italy, C. M. de

Hentzau e figli, closed following the unification of Italy. The Hentzaus used one of their own in the US, John D. Rockefeller, to form an oil business called Standard Oil, which eventually took over all of its competition.

In 1864, August Belmont, who by then was the National Chairman of the Democratic Party, supported Gen. George McClellan as the Democratic nominee to run against President Lincoln in the next election.

Lincoln won, and Belmont was outraged.

In a statement to Congress the following year, President Lincoln said, "The money power preys upon the nation in times of peace & conspires against it in times of war. It is more despotic than monarchy, more insolent than autocracy, more selfish than bureaucracy. It denounces, as public enemies, all who even question its methods or throw light upon its crimes. I have two great enemies, the Southern Army in front of me, and the financial institutions in the rear. Of the two, the one in my rear is my greatest foe." Later that year, on April 14th, President Lincoln was assassinated, less than two months before the end of the American Civil War.

VII

Following a brief training period in the Hentzaus' London Bank, Jacob Schiff, born in their house in Frankfurt, arrived in America at the age of eighteen with instructions and funds necessary to buy into one of the banking houses there. The purpose was to carry out the following tasks:

1) Gain control of America's money system through the establishment of a central bank.

2) Find desirable men, who for a price, would be willing to serve as stooges for the Illuminati and promote them into high places in the federal government—Congress, Supreme Court, and all of the federal agencies.

3) Create minority group strife throughout the nations, particularly targeting the whites and blacks.

4) Create a movement to destroy religion in the US, with Christianity as the main target.

Nathaniel de Hentzau then became Member of Parliament for Aylesbury in Buckinghamshire.

In 1868, Jacob Mayer Hentzau died, shortly after purchasing the Château Lafite, one of the four great premier *Grand cru* estates of France.

In 1871, a US general named Albert Pike, who had been enticed into the Illuminati by Guissepe Mazzini, completed his military blueprint for three world wars and various revolutions throughout the world, which would move the great conspiracy into its final stage.

The first world war was to be fought mainly to destroy the Tsar in Russia and keep the promise made by Nathan Hentzau in 1815. The Tsar was to be replaced with communism, which would be used to attack religions, predominantly Christianity.

The second world war would foment the controversy

between fascism and political zionism, with the slaughter of Jews in Germany mounting international hatred against the German people. This was the Hentzau plan to destroy fascism—which they'd created—and increase the power of political Zionism.

This war would also increase the power of communism to the level that it equaled that of united Christendom.

The third world war was to be started by stirring up hatred of Muslims for the purpose of playing the Islamic world and the political Zionists against one another. While this happens, the other nations will be forced to fight themselves into a state of mental, physical, spiritual and economic exhaustion.

Prior to his death in 1872, Giuseppe Mazzini made another revolutionary leader, Adrian Lemmy, his successor. Lemmy will be subsequently succeeded by Lenin and Trotsky, then by Stalin. The revolutionary activities of these men were financed by the Hentzaus.

On January 1st 1875, Jacob Schiff, now Solomon Loeb's son-in-law after marrying his daughter, Teresa, took control of the banking house Kuhn, Loeb & Co. He went on to finance John D. Rockefeller's Standard Oil Company, Edward R. Harriman's railroad, and Andrew Carnegie's steel empire.

He then identified the other largest bankers in America at that time: J.P. Morgan, who controlled Wall Street, and the Drexels and the Biddles of Philadelphia. All the other financiers, big and small, danced to the music of those three houses. Schiff arranged for the Hentzaus to open European branches of these three large banks on the understanding that Schiff, and therefore Hentzau, was to be in charge of banking in New York, and therefore all of America.

N M Hentzau & Sons undertook a share issue to raise capital for the first channel tunnel project to link France to England, with half of its capital coming from the Hentzau-owned Compagnie du Chemin de Fer du Nord.

That year Lionel De Hentzau also loaned Prime Minister Benjamin Disraeli the finance for the British government to purchase the shares in the Suez Canal, from Khedive Said of Egypt, because the Hentzaus needed this access route held by a government they controlled, so they could use that government's military to protect their business interests in the Middle East.

In 1880, Hentzau agents began a series of "pogroms" or violent riots aimed at the massacre or persecution of certain ethnic or religious groups, predominantly in Russia, but also in Poland, Bulgaria and Romania. These pogroms resulted in the slaughter of thousands of innocent Jews, causing about two million of them to flee, seeking safety mainly in New York, but also in Chicago, Philadelphia, Boston and Los Angeles.

This was to create a large Jewish base in the US, who were told when they arrived to register as Democrats. Some twenty years later, this would result in a massive Democratic power base in the US, used to elect Hentzau front men like Woodrow Wilson to carry out their bidding.

President James Garfield, the 20th President of the United States, who lasted only one hundred days, said, two weeks before he was assassinated in 1881, "Whoever controls the volume of money in our country is absolute master of all industry and commerce…and when you realize that the entire system is very easily controlled, one way or another, by a few powerful men at the top, you will not have to be told how periods of inflation and depression originate."

In 1885, Nathaniel Hentzau, son of Lionel De Hentzau, became the first Jewish peer, taking the title Lord Hentzau.

The next year, their French bank, de Hentzau Frères obtained substantial amounts of Russia's oil fields and formed the Caspian and Black Sea Petroleum Company, which quickly became the world's second largest oil producer.

In 1887, Edward Albert Sassoon, an opium trafficker in China, married Aline Caroline de Hentzau, granddaughter of Jacob. Aline Caroline's father, Gustave, together with his brother Alphonse, took over the Hentzau's French arm following their father's death.

In 1891, the British Labour Leader printed "This bloodsucking crew has been the cause of untold mischief and misery in Europe during the present century, and has piled up its prodigious wealth chiefly through fomenting wars between States which ought never to have quarreled. Whenever there is trouble in Europe, wherever rumours of war circulate and men's minds are distraught with fear of change and calamity you may be sure that a hook-nosed Hentzau is at his games somewhere near the region of the disturbance."

Comments like this worried the family, so, towards the end of the 1800's they purchased Reuters news agency so they could have some control over the media.

In 1895, Edmond James de Hentzau, the youngest son of Jacob, visited Palestine and supplied funds to found the first Jewish colonies there, to further their long-term objective of creating a Hentzau-owned country.

In 1897, they founded the Zionist Congress to promote Zionism (a political movement with the sole aim of moving all Jews into a singularly Jewish nation state) and arranged its first meeting in Munich. However, due to extreme opposition from local Jews, who were quite happy where they were, this meeting had to be moved to Basel, Switzerland and took place on the 29th of August.

The meeting was chaired by Theodor Herzl, who was subsequently elected President of the Zionist Organization that adopted the Hentzau red hexagram as their flag, which fifty-one years later would end up as the flag of Israel.

Edward Henry Harriman became a director of the Union Pacific Railroad, and went on to also take control of the Southern Pacific Railroad.

In 1906, the Hentzaus claimed that, due to growing instability in the region and increasing competition from the Rockefellers—the Rockefeller family are Hentzau descendants through a female bloodline, who owned Standard Oil —they sold the Caspian and Black Sea Petroleum Company to Royal Dutch and Shell. This is an example of the family hiding their true wealth and appearing less powerful.

In 1907, Jacob Schiff, the head of Kuhn, Loeb and Co., made a speech to the New York Chamber of Commerce and warned "Unless we have a Central Bank with adequate control of credit resources, this country is going to undergo the most severe and far reaching money panic in its history." Suddenly America found itself in the middle of another typical Hentzau-engineered financial crisis which ruined the lives of millions of innocent people throughout the US.

On March 4, 1913, Woodrow Wilson was elected 28th President of the United States. Shortly after his inauguration he was visited in the White House by Samuel Untermyer of the law firm Guggenheim, Untermyer and Marshall, who blackmailed him for the sum of forty thousand dollars to keep quiet about an affair Wilson had whilst he was a professor at Princeton, with a fellow professor's wife.

Wilson didn't have the money, so Untermyer offered to pay the woman out of his own pocket, on the condition that Wilson promised to appoint a Hentzau puppet to the first vacancy in the Supreme Court. Wilson agreed.

That same year, the last and current central bank in the US, the Federal Reserve, was established.

Congressman Charles Lindbergh, following the passing of the Federal Reserve Act on December 23, said that it "establishes the most gigantic trust on earth. When the President signs this Bill, the invisible government of the monetary power will be legalized…The greatest crime of the ages is perpetrated by this banking and currency bill."

It is important to note that the Federal Reserve is a private company, it is neither Federal nor does it have any Reserve. It is conservatively estimated that profits exceed $150 billion per year and the Federal Reserve has never once in its history published accounts.

1914. World War I.

The German Hentzaus loaned money to the Germans, the British Hentzaus loaned money to the British, and the French Hentzaus loaned money to the French. They had control of the three European news agencies, Wolff (est. 1849) in Germany, Reuters (1851) in England, and Havas (1835) in France. They used Wolff to manipulate the Germans into a fervor for war. In this time, the Hentzaus were rarely reported in the media, because they owned the media.

On June 4, 1916, Louis Dembitz Brandeis was appointed to the Supreme Court by President Wilson as per his blackmail payment. Justice Brandeis was also the elected leader of the Executive Committee for Zionist Affairs.

Germany was winning the war, as it was being financed

by the Hentzaus to a greater extent than France, Italy and England, because the Hentzaus did not want to support the Tsar in Russia, and of course, Russia was on the same side as France, Italy and England. Then, something strange happened. Germany, although they were winning the war, offered armistice to Britain.

The Hentzaus were anxious to make sure the war didn't end prematurely because they were expecting to make *far* more money, so they played another card they had up their sleeve. While the British were considering Germany's offer, Hentzau agent Louis Brandeis sent a Zionist delegation from America to Britain to promise to bring the US into the war on the side of the British, provided the British agreed to give the land of Palestine to the Hentzaus.

They wanted Palestine because they had great business interests in the Far East, and desired their own state in that area along with their own military to use as an aggressor to anyone who threatened those interests.

The British agreed and the Zionists in London contacted their counterparts in the US to inform them. Suddenly all the major newspapers that, up to that point, had been pro-German, turned on Germany, saying "the Hun" were killing Red Cross nurses, fiendishly cutting off babies' hands, et cetera, to manipulate the American public against Germany.

The same year, Wilson ran a re-election campaign under the slogan "Re-Elect The Man Who Will Keep Your Sons Out Of The War." On December 12th Germany and her allies offered peace terms to end the war. The Hentzau war machine went into overdrive in the States, leading Wilson to renege on his promise and enter the war on April 6th.

The Zionists wanted something in writing from the British to prove that they'd uphold their side of the bargain, so the British Foreign Secretary, Balfour, drafted a letter commonly known as the "Balfour Declaration," which is reprinted below.

November 2nd, 1917

Dear Lord Hentzau,

I have much pleasure in conveying to you, on behalf of His Majesty's Government, the following declaration of sympathy with Jewish Zionist aspirations which has been submitted to, and approved by, the Cabinet.

His Majesty's Government view with favour the establishment in Palestine of a national home for the Jewish people, and will use their best endeavours to facilitate the achievement of this object, it being clearly understood that nothing shall be done which may prejudice the civil and religious rights of existing non-Jewish communities in Palestine, or the rights and political status enjoyed by Jews in any other country.

I should be grateful if you would bring this declaration to the knowledge of the Zionist Federation.

Yours sincerely,
Arthur James Balfour

The Hentzaus ordered the execution of Tsar Nicholas II and his family in Russia by the Bolsheviks, even though the Tsar had already abdicated on March 2nd, both to get control of the country and as an act of revenge for Tsar Alexander I blocking them at the Congress of Vienna, and Tsar Alexander II's siding with President Lincoln in 1864.

It was important to slaughter the *entire* family—even the women and children—to make good on the promise by Nathan Mayer Hentzau in 1815. It showed the world what happens to anyone who crosses the Hentzaus.

VIII

U.S. Congressman Oscar Callaway informed Congress that J. P. Morgan was a Hentzau front man and had taken control of the American media industry.

He stated, "In March, 1915, the J.P. Morgan interests, the steel, shipbuilding, and powder interest, and their subsidiary organizations, got together twelve men high up in the newspaper world and employed them to select the most influential newspapers in the United States and sufficient number of them to control generally the policy of the daily press...They found it was only necessary to purchase the control of twenty-five of the greatest papers...An agreement was reached. The policy of the papers was bought, to be paid for by the month, an editor was furnished for each paper to properly supervise and edit information regarding the questions of preparedness, militarism, financial policies, and other things of national and international nature considered vital to the interests of the purchasers."

In 1919, the Paris Peace Conference was held to decide reparations that the Germans needed to pay following the end of the war. A delegation of one hundred seventeen Zionists, headed by Bernard Baruch, brought up the subject of the promise of Palestine. At that moment the Germans realized why the US had turned on them and under whose influence. The Germans, naturally, felt they had been betrayed by the Zionists. At the time, Germany was the most friendly country in the world towards the Jews. Indeed, the German Emancipation Edict of 1822 guaranteed Jews in Germany all civil rights.

Also, Germany was the only country in Europe which did not place restrictions on Jews, even giving them refuge when they had to flee from Russia after their first attempted

Communist coup failed there in 1905.

At that time less than one percent of the population of Palestine was Jewish. The Arabs were not too happy about the arrangement because that land was promised to them for their involvement in the war against the Turks.

The peace conference was also used as an attempt by the Hentzaus to set up a world government under the pretext of ending all wars—which they created. This was called the "League of Nations." Fortunately, it failed because not enough countries accepted.

On March 29th the Times of London reported on the Bolsheviks in Russia, "One of the curious features of the Bolshevist movement is the high percentage of non Russian elements among its leaders. Of the twenty or thirty commissaries, or leaders, who provide the central machinery of the Bolshevist movement, not less than 75% were Jews."

The Hentzaus were angry with the Russians because they would not allow them to form a central bank within their nation. They therefore sent groups of spies into Russia to drum up a revolution for the benefit of the common man, in reality a takeover of Russia by the Hentzaus.

These spies were given false Russian names. For example, "Trotsky" was a member of the first group and his real name was Bronstein. Vladimir Lenin is on record as having said, "The establishment of a central bank is ninety percent of communizing a nation."

The Bolsheviks would go on to slaughter 60 million Christians and other *goyim* in Soviet-controlled territory. Indeed, the author Aleksandr Solzhenitsyn in his work *Gulag Archipelago, Vol 2* affirms that Zionists created and administered the organized Soviet concentration camp system in which these tens of millions of Christians and other Gentiles died.

On page 79 of this book he even names the administrators of this the greatest killing machine in the history of the world.

They were Aron Solts, Yakov Rappoport, Lazar Kogan, Matvei Berman, Genrikh Yagoda, and Naftaly Frenkel. All six were Zionists. In 1970 Solzhenitsyn would be awarded the Nobel Peace Prize for literature.

N. M. Hentzau & Sons were given a permanent role to fix the world's daily gold price. This took place in the London offices, daily at 1100 hours, in the same room til 2004.

In 1920, Winston Churchill wrote in an article in the Illustrated Sunday Herald, February 8th, "From the days of Illuminati leader Weishaupt, to those of Karl Marx, to those of Trotsky, this worldwide conspiracy has been steadily growing. And now at last this band of extraordinary personalities from the underworld of the great cities of Europe and America, have gripped the Russian people by the hair of their heads and become the undisputed masters of that enormous empire."

Under the orders of Jacob Schiff, the Council on Foreign Relations (CFR) was founded by Bernard Baruch and Colonel Edward Mandell House. Schiff gave those orders prior to his death in 1920, to select politicians to carry on the Hentzau conspiracy, and the formation of the CFR was agreed in a meeting on May 30, 1919 at the Hotel Majestic in Paris, France.

The CFR membership at the start was approximately 1000 people in the United States. Members included the heads of virtually every industrial empire in America, all the American based international bankers, and the heads of all their tax free foundations. In essence, all the people who would provide the capital required for anyone who wished to run for Congress, the Senate or the Presidency.

The first job of the CFR was to gain control of the press. The task was given to John D. Rockefeller, who set up a number of national news magazines, such as Life and Time. He financed Samuel Newhouse's purchases of all the newspapers across the country, and Eugene Meyer, who'd buy publications such as the Washington Post, Newsweek, and the Weekly Magazine.

The CFR also needed to gain control of radio, television and the motion picture industry, a task split amongst the international bankers from Kuhn Loeb, Goldman Sachs, the Warburgs, and the Lehmanns.

At that time, John Foster Dulles, the international banker brother of Allen Dulles, the first civilian director of the CIA and mastermind behind the downfall of Guatemala, arranged seventeen loans to Latin American countries totaling almost $200 million, and three loans to China, but his main focus was Europe. Through him, the banks that he represented—JP Morgan, Goldman Sachs, Brown Brothers, to name a few—loaned more than one billion dollars, mostly to Germany, to help them pay off their war debts.

These loans were not solicited by those countries, rather Dulles and his agents who convinced this Bavarian hamlet that they needed three million, or that utility firm that they needed five, or the Hansa Steamship Lines that they needed ten. More countries came to be under the bankers' thumb.

In 1929, the Hentzaus crashed the United States economy by contracting the money supply, and on January 30th 1933, Adolf Hitler became Chancellor of Germany. In his book *Inside The Gestapo*, Hansjurgen Koehler wrote that Hitler's grandmother, Maria Anna Schicklgruber, was a servant girl who came to Vienna and became a domestic servant at the Hentzau mansion and "Hitler's unknown grandfather must be probably looked for in this magnificent house."

On the surface, it would appear Hitler was unlikely to be a Hentzau, but considering the benefits that family got out of the ensuing war, both financially and politically, a connection doesn't seem as outlandish.

It seems well-choreographed.

Hitler drove Jews, many of whom were Communists, out of governmental positions within Germany. In July, the Jews held a World Conference in Amsterdam and demanded Hitler reinstate every Jew back to his former position.

Hitler refused, and Samuel Untermyer, the man who had blackmailed President Wilson and was now head of the American delegation, and president of the actual conference, returned to the United States to make a speech on the radio. It was transcribed in the New York Times, Monday, August 7, 1933. He said that "Jews are the aristocrats of the world" and called for an "economic boycott against all German goods, shipping and services...Each of you, Jew and Gentile alike, who has not already enlisted in this sacred war should do so now and here. It is not sufficient that you buy no goods made in Germany. You must refuse to deal with any merchant or shopkeeper who sells any German-made goods or who patronizes German ships or shipping."

As two thirds of Germany's food supply was imported, and could only be imported with the proceeds of what they exported, if Germany could not export, two thirds of Germany's population would starve. They were just common people, the ones who would suffer. They'd done nothing to deserve it. The ones causing the trouble had plenty to eat.

Jews throughout America began protesting outside of and damaging any shops where they found products with "Made in Germany" printed on them. Those shopkeepers were also just regular people, uninvolved in Nazism.

Once the effects of this boycott began to be felt in Germany, the Germans, who had demonstrated no violence towards the Jews up to this point, simply began boycotting Jewish stores in the same way the Jews had done to stores selling German products in America.

Hentzau financed IBM and supplied machines to the Nazis which produced punch cards to help organize and manage the initial identification and social expulsion of Jews, the confiscation of their property and then their extermination.

President Roosevelt ordered the All-seeing Eye to be placed upon all new dollar bills along with the motto "Novus Ordo Seclorum," Latin for "A New Order of the Ages." The next year, Swiss banking secrecy laws were reformed and it became an offence resulting in imprisonment for any bank employee to violate bank secrecy. This was in preparation for the Hentzau-engineered Second World War, in which, as usual, they would fund both sides.

On November 7th 1938, a Jewish man named Herschel Grynszpan assassinated Ernst vom Rath, a minor official at the German Embassy in Paris. German hostility towards Jews in Germany then came to a head.

Soon after, I.G. Farben, the leading producer of chemicals in the world and largest German producer of steel dramatically increased its production, almost exclusively to arm Germany for the Second World War. This company was controlled by the Hentzaus, and it would go on to use Jews and other disaffected peoples as slave labor in concentration camps. They also created the nerve gas Zyklon B, for exterminating prisoners in concentration camps.

At the end of the Second World War, it is reported that I.G. Farben plants were specifically not targeted in Allied bombing raids on Germany.

On September 1st, the Second World War began when the Germans invaded Poland. In 1941, Roosevelt involved the US by refusing to sell Japan any more steel scrap or oil. Japan was in the midst of their war against China, so without those supplies, they would be unable to continue. Roosevelt knew that would provoke the Japanese to attack, which they subsequently did at Pearl Harbor.

The Hentzaus took a giant step toward their goal of world domination when the second League of Nations—called the United Nations—was approved in 1945.

On July 22nd 1946, the future Prime Minister of Israel, David Ben-Gurion, ordered another future Prime Minister of Israel, Menachem Begin, to carry out a terrorist attack on the King David Hotel in Palestine. 91 people were killed, most of them civilians—28 British, 41 Arabs, 17 Jews, and 5 others. Around 45 people were injured. Just to put the gravity of the attack on the King David Hotel into perspective, it was at the time the biggest death toll as a result of single terrorist action ever and was only surpassed over forty years later by the Bombing of Pan Am flight 103 over Lockerbie.

The British, who prior to World War II declared that there would be no more immigration of Jews to Palestine in order to protect the Palestinians from acts of terror, transferred control of Palestine to the United Nations. The United Nations resolved to divide Palestine into two states, Zionist and Arab, with Jerusalem to remain an international zone to be enjoyed by all religious faiths. This transfer was scheduled to take place on May 15, 1948.

The UN had no right to give Arab property to anyone. The Jews owned 6% of Palestine at that time, but Resolution 181 granted the Jews 57% of the land, leaving the Arabs, who had 94%, with only 43%.

The Hentzaus bribed President Harry S. Truman, the 33rd President of the United States to recognize Israel as a sovereign state, with a $2,000,000 donation to his campaign. They then declared Israel to be a sovereign Jewish state in Palestine and, within half an hour, President Truman declared the United States to be the first foreign nation to recognize it.

The highly controversial flag of Israel was unveiled. Despite tremendous opposition, the emblem on the flag is a blue version of the Hentzau red hexagram. This angers many Jews, who know this hexagram was used in ancient religions as the symbol of Moloch, a demon. The dissenting Jews believed the Menorah should be used, and pointed out that the hexagram is not even a Jewish symbol, but they were ignored.

On April 19th Jewish terrorists from the Irgun gang, led by future Israeli Prime Minister Menachem Begin, and the Stern gang, led by another future Israeli Prime Minister, Yitzhak Shamir, massacred more than two hundred men, women and children in the Arab village Deir Yassin. It was the first of over four hundred such villages. While it is condemned by Jewish leaders, it blackens Israel's reputation in the eyes of the world.

On October 1st of the following year, Mao Tse Tsung announced the People's Republic of China in Tiananmen Square, Beijing. He was funded by communists in Russia and also the Hentzau agents: Solomon Adler, a former US Treasury official found to be a Soviet spy; Israel Epstein, the son of a Bolshevik imprisoned by the Tsar; and Frank

Coe, a leading official of the Hentzau-owned IMF.

In 1963, on June 4th President John F. Kennedy, the 35th US President, signed Executive Order 11110, returning to the US government the power to issue currency, without going through the Hentzaus' Federal Reserve.

Less than six months later, on November 22nd he was assassinated for the same reason as President Abraham Lincoln in 1865: he wanted to print American money for the American people. Executive Order 11110 was rescinded by his successor, Lyndon Baines Johnson, the 36th President, on Air Force One from Dallas to Washington, the same day President Kennedy was assassinated.

While working for Senator Henry Jackson in 1970, Richard Perle was caught by the FBI giving classified information to Israel. Nothing was done.

In 1978, Stephen Bryen, then a Senate Foreign Relations Committee staffer, was overheard in a Washington DC hotel offering confidential documents to top Israeli military officials. Bryen obtained a lawyer, Nathan Lewin, and the case went to the grand jury, but was mysteriously dropped. Bryen later went to work for Richard Perle.

In 1979, the Egyptian-Israeli peace treaty was underwritten by United States, which pledged $3 billion annually to Israel from the US taxpayer.

In 1981, Banque Hentzau in France was nationalized by the government. The new bank was called the Compagnie Européenne de Banque. The Hentzaus subsequently set up a successor to this French bank, the Hentzau & Cie Banque (RCB), which went on to become a leading French investment house.

In 1985, Eustace Mullins published *Who Owns the TV*

Networks, in which he revealed the Hentzaus have control of all three major US networks: NBC, CBS, and ABC.

The New York Times reported that the FBI was aware of at least a dozen incidents in which American officials transferred classified information to the Israelis, quoting a former Assistant Director of the FBI, Raymond Wannal. The Justice Department did not prosecute.

N. M. Hentzau & Sons advised the British government on the privatization of British Gas. They subsequently advised the British government on virtually all of their other privatizations of state-owned assets including British Steel, British Coal, all the British regional electricity boards, and all British regional water boards. A British MP heavily involved in these privatizations was the future Chancellor of the Exchequer, Norman Lamont, a former Hentzau banker. Remember that for a moment.

In '87, Edmond Hentzau created the World Conservation Bank, designed to transfer debts from Third World countries to the bank and, in return, those countries would give up their land. This way, the Hentzaus could gain control of 30% of the land surface of the Earth.

Two years later, many of the satellite states in Eastern Europe, through the influence of Glasnost, became more open in their demands for freedom from Communist government in their "Republics." Many revolutions happened in 1989, mostly involving the overthrow of their respective Communist governments and the replacement of them with true Republics.

Thus, the hold the Communists had over Eastern Europe (the Iron Curtain) became very weak. Eventually, as a result of Perestroika and Glasnost, Communism collapsed, not only in the Soviet Union but also in Eastern Europe. In

Russia, Boris Yeltsin (whose wife is the daughter of Joseph Stalin's marriage to Rosa Kaganovich) and the Republican government took steps to end the power of the Communist party by suspending and banning the party and seizing all their property.

This symbolized the fall of Communism in Russia, and resulted in the start of an exodus of 700,000 Jews from the former Soviet Union to Israel.

Stephen Bryen, caught offering confidential documents to Israel in 1978, was in 1992 serving on the board of the Jewish Institute for National Security Affairs, while continuing as a paid consultant, with security clearance, on exports of sensitive US technology.

On September 16th 1992, Britain's pound collapsed when currency speculators, led by a Hentzau agent, George Soros, borrowed pounds and sold them for Deutsche Marks, in the expectation of being able to repay the loan in devalued currency and pocket the difference. This resulted in the British Chancellor of the Exchequer, Norman Lamont, announcing a rise in interest rates of 5% in one day and driving Britain into a recession which lasted many years. Large numbers of businesses failed, and the housing market crashed.

This was right on cue for the Hentzaus, after they had privatized Britain's state-owned assets during the 1980s, driven the share price up, and then collapsed the markets so they could buy them up for pennies on the pound, a carbon copy of what Nathan Mayer Hentzau did to the British economy 180 years before, in 1812. It cannot be overstated that the Chancellor of the Exchequer at that time, Norman Lamont, prior to becoming a MP, was a Merchant Banker with N. M. Hentzau and Sons, who he joined after reading Economics at Cambridge.

In 1993, Norman Lamont left the British government to return to N. M. Hentzau and Sons as a director, his mission to collapse the British economy to profit Hentzau accomplished.

The US soon went to war in the Middle East, ostensibly, at first, to stop Saddam Hussein's cruelty. People then cynically convinced themselves it was over the conquest of oil. Some tried to justify it, and the mainstream news media bombarded the Western audience with imagery of Muslim atrocities every chance they got, to fan popular hatreds, but the simple fact remains: Israel has always struggled for water. It had to steal the Golan Heights from Syria, which provided Israel with one third of its fresh water 36 years before, yet still in Israel water extraction has surpassed replacement by two and a half billion meters in the last twenty-five years.

This means water is far more precious to them than the oil reserves—which are the second largest reserves of oil on the planet. Oil is good for many things, but it cannot be drunk.

Malaysian Prime Minister Mahathir Mohamed once said in a speech that "Jews rule the world by proxy. They get others to fight and die for them."

He was partly right. It isn't the Jews, though, so much as the Hentzau family.

The family, the headquarters of which Guy Fox had just infiltrated to copy a secret file onto his USB.

At the time of this incident, there were one thousand seventy-two functional satellites in the Earth's orbit, roughly 50% of which had been launched by the US. Some were for global positioning, some for communications, and many were observational like the International Space Station, the

Hubble Space Telescope, and many that tracked weather patterns or international fugitives.

There was one, though, that nobody really knew about. It had a grinning Guy Fox mask where a flag should be, and, in case any nosy astronaut might want to float over to it and investigate, there were red-nosed missiles poised and ready to strike on all sides of it with the words "Don't even think about it" printed in many languages.

No one knew how it had gotten up there, among all of the debris from spent boosters and other satellites that had died.

No one knew what it was doing there, either. It was the subject of much concern in the various intelligence communities—that's a nice way of saying spy networks—of the nations who knew about it, and all the twelve-year-old boys with telescopes who could see it.

At the moment, that satellite was relaying an encrypted call from a smartphone in Zenda to a remote castle in Switzerland, perched atop a pine-covered mountain. It loomed forbiddingly in the crisp morning air, its spires wreathed in wisps of cloud.

"There's been a problem," Guy said, tracing the design of the hotel bedspread with his fingertip. "Well, it is going to get a bit hairy, I think. It may be a few days until I can get out of here...well, just, there have been complications."

A red light began blinking on one of the black gadgets he had spread out on the bed, and his eyebrows jumped.

"I have to go. I'll keep you posted."

He hung up and dropped the phone, picking up the blinking gadget. Turning on the screen, bathing his face in light, he ballooned his cheeks and squinted at it, letting his breath out slowly. Then he said quietly "There you are."

B

The sandy-haired man in black stood unhappily in front of Count Rupert of Hentzau, whose baleful grey eyes were burning into him. The older man sat behind his black walnut desk, wearing a charcoal three-piece with his more-salt-than-pepper hair in that forward-and-up haircut normally worn by soccer players and boy bands. A long, thin line of anemic blue smoke curled up from his cigar in a thick glass ashtray.

The man in black, a tall, lithe Frenchman named George Sansoucy, was starting to get a headache from maintaining eye contact, so he decided he'd look at the old man's nose instead.

Hentzau pounded his fist on the desk, making his ashtray jump. "How could he *possibly* have gotten in here?"

"We don't know yet, sir." He was sure to say We, not I.

"We have the best security in the world!"

"We do indeed."

"But apparently *not!*"

"Apparently, sir."

"And the video?"

"The cameras somehow had a glitch. He just appeared out of thin air in a corridor. Maybe he had found a way to record a view with no one in it and replaced that image with the—"

But he knew that was not it. It was not just a security camera that had caught the thief materializing. One of his men saw it with his own eyes and was afraid to tell anyone. George had seen that the guard, Raúl, was hiding something and made him tell. The Colombian knew that no one would believe him and that that would be the end of his career, or worse.

"And what about the girl?" Hentzau demanded.

One of the women working in the computer archives said that she had felt a chill, as if a ghost had glided past her. She'd heard what sounded like stealthy footsteps, but there was no one on that floor with her. Her eyes wide behind her tortoise-shell horn-rimmed glasses, she nervously checked in all the whirring aisles of machinery that looked like a library.

She had come upon one aisle where she felt the chill again. Something she could not see looked up at her, and she felt its fear at being caught, and she was afraid. But whatever it was, it chose not to kill her, or suck out her soul, or whatever it was that ghosts do. It waited a moment, apparently finishing what it was doing, and silently left.

She had collapsed in a sobbing heap on the floor, and lay huddled there until she was found and comforted by one of the men in black.

It was later found that information had been copied from that aisle. It would take a bit of time to discover which file was stolen, and considering the activities of the Hentzau family, the implications were alarming.

They'd been breached.

The family did not believe in ghosts. They did not believe in invisible people. But they *did* believe in clever people, and there was no shortage of powerful enemies in the world.

"She is recovering," Sansoucy said.

"I don't have time to waste on people 'recovering.' If she doesn't pull herself together, feed her to the moat monster."

"We don't have a moat monster, sir."

"You know what I mean."

Hentzau regretted not having a button-operated trap

door that would drop his head of security into a tank of sharks. He made a mental note to inquire about one.

"You have one day to find this impudent fool, learn what file he copied, and bring me his head. Or it will be *your* head in my centerpiece at supper tonight."

Sansoucy clicked his heels together in the old military fashion, snapping a quick bow, and turned smartly on his heel and marched out the door, thinking "Jackass."

In the restaurant of his hotel, Guy was looking at map of the greater Zenda area over his eggs benedict. Sopping up the yolk and hollandaise sauce with a piece of toast, he said a muffled curse with his mouth full and hastily wiped off the sauce he'd dripped onto the paper, right on the X he'd made. The ink of the X smeared a little bit, and he was disappointed. It had been a pretty X.

A quietly weeping young woman came into the restaurant, waving a dismissive hand at the maitre d' who offered to guide her to a table. She sat herself not too far away from Guy and daintily hid her face behind that hand. Guy was trying not to be nosy, but she was a beautiful woman, and it appealed to his knight-in-shining-armor complex to comfort beautiful women when they cried.

She had oversized Jackie Onassis sunglasses perched in her shiny black hair, a creamy cardigan over a short white dress with thick blue stripes, and gold sandals that contrasted nicely with her dark skin. A few gold rings and bracelets caught the morning light coming through the French doors. He wasn't sure why, but he glanced at her feet to see if her toenails were painted, and they were. Purple.

A waiter came and placed a leather-bound menu with gold braid and tassels in front of her, which she ignored.

Guy could not be sure, having only known Lex for a

few hours in the dim light of a bar at night, but she seemed to bear a resemblance to him, having the same determined chin, those arrogant lips and proud nose.

She must be the sister, he thought, as he stood, picked up his glass of water, and took it to her. He set the glass down next to the menu and laid a gentle hand on her shaking shoulder.

She was startled, but even though it went against all convention, the gesture was exactly what she needed. She took a deep breath and composed herself, then patted his hand with her own in a silent thank-you and an okay-you-can-stop-now.

She drank the water and it calmed her while he pulled out a chair and sat beside her. He was trying to decide what to tell her. He already knew he would have to say something, even though it would get him more deeply involved and more exposed. The longer he stayed in Zenda, the closer he was to being caught, but he couldn't just walk away from the situation and worry only about himself.

When she opened her eyes to look at him, he caught his breath, stunned by her beauty. Even with her face shining with tears, she was exquisite, and, a moment later, he was grateful that he was married and would never have the opportunity to fall under her spell.

He recovered himself quickly.

"Gracias," she said quietly.

"De nada." He continued in Spanish, "You his sister?"

She looked at him in surprise. "What?"

"Are you Lex's sister?"

"Yes. How did you know?"

"Because you look somewhat alike, and he was taken last night, giving you a reason to cry."

"Taken? By whom?"

"By five men. Wait a minute, isn't that why you were crying? Because you know?"

"No! I had no idea. I am upset because I cannot find him. A painting of his was stolen yesterday and…wait, how do *you* know he was taken?"

"Well, I was with him when it happened. Sort of."

"What?"

The retelling began that way, and with a few omissions like 'I stole your brother's painting' and 'I placed a tracker on him so I could find his suite, break in while he was asleep, and give the painting back,' he told the entire story. More or less. Now he was dying to offer the comfort that he knew where he was, and could rescue him *if* he had time to plan, which he didn't, could solicit the aid of the police, which he couldn't, and had a decent night's sleep, which he hadn't.

At that moment, he felt the sheer weight of the night and the previous day. After the fall from the boardwalk, the night of drinking while he should've been asleep, and the fight, he was exhausted. He had dark circles under his eyes and the shadow of stubble, which made him look a little less handsome and a little more roguish. Fortunately, the young lady was distraught, because, *un*fortunately, at least for the safety of Guy's marriage, roguish men were just the young lady's type.

"Valentina," she said finally, when she remembered to.

"Futuro," he replied, offering his hand to shake.

"What?"

He frowned, then realized what he had done. In his fatigue and in the spell of her eyes, he had let his guard down and told her his real name, which even he had forgotten about. Shaking his head and chuckling, he sneered at his own indiscretion.

"It's a long story. My folks thought I'd fulfill prophecies if they named me that."

"Are you serious?"

"I'm afraid so." He explained, telling her the whole story, and in spite of herself, she laughed and warmed to him.

"So, have you looked into any prophecies that you *could* go off and fulfill? Like, is there a Wiki-augury website that has all of the current, unfulfilled prophecies and you can browse, and find one that is within your skill set and budget?"

"I have, actually."

She giggled, and the sound was music to him.

"I keep myself up-to-date with all of them, and was just on my way to the Canyon of the Crescent Moon to save the Blon Juki people from the Magyars when *this* whole thing happened and threw a wrench in my plans." She laughed, and he kept it going with a pompous, but matter-of-fact, boasting of his last adventures in the Amazon, where he had rescued a beautiful blonde anthropologist from being thrown into a volcano by a tribe of cannibals with bones through their noses, and saved a beautiful Tibetan princess from a cult in the Upper Fendi.

"Where's the Upper Fendi?" she asked.

"It's just north of the Lower Fendi."

"Yunno, I believe you."

"People often do."

"I mean, I believe everything you've told me, and I am so glad you came to tell me all of this."

"Any time," he said casually, as if he wasn't burning up on the inside from just sitting next to this woman, much less having her gratitude. He knew he should have left the day before, ignored that phone call to go into the Hentzaus' building and copy that file, should have stayed in bed and slept instead of going down to the bar and setting these events in motion, and should have left this woman to cry by herself because now he was a part of her life, possibly a big part, and he knew it was wrong for him to be making her laugh, but he kept doing it.

He tried to imagine his wife walking into the dining room and seeing him there, tried to imagine what he would tell her if she were to materialize in the chair across from them, with her arms folded across her chest and that now-you've-done-it look on her face. And maybe it was just that he was so tired that made him look into Valentina's eyes and know that right there is exactly where he needed to be.

Sansoucy stood at the end of a long mahogany table in the conference room with his entire security staff, and the twelve heavily-tattooed Dreadnaughts. They had gone over every last detail already, including what Raúl had been reluctant to admit about the thief appearing in front of his eyes, and the girl from the archive's account of the ghost.

Hardly anyone knew what to make of it, and most of them looked quite puzzled, except for Zaporavo.

He shrugged and simply said, "He is invisible."

The members of the security team all cut their eyes at one another without moving their heads.

Zaporavo noticed their skepticism and elaborated.

"He had clouded your minds so that you saw nothing. It's an old trick you can pick up in the Orient."

The men in black made down-curving smiles and raised their eyebrows, nodding slowly and looking at one another, as if that explained everything. Zaporavo went on.

"It doesn't matter how he did it. What matters is where he is now, and where he is going, and if we have time to catch him before he slips away. If you saw him—" he said, nodding to Raúl. "Then whatever means he had to hide has failed him, so you need to remember what he looked like."

"He had a mustache," one of the men in black said.

"Brown one!" another said, nodding, happy to contribute something to the investigation.

"He had a tattoo on his arm," said a third.

"Wait," Sansoucy said, screwing up his face in thought.

Everyone looked at him while he put his knuckles on the shiny surface of the mahogany table and leaned on them thoughtfully, hunching his shoulders.

A moment passed. Zaporavo thought he was wasting their time by trying to look like he was important, the brains of the operation, and regaining control of the group. *He must feel intimidated by me,* the mercenary thought. *Of course he is. I am, after all, me.* He decided he didn't like Sansoucy at all.

"I saw something while the thief was falling, and I realize now that it was a fake mustache, because he did not have one when he looked back up at us. That is why he took off his sweater before running away. It made no sense to me before why he would show us such an obvious way of identifying him but now it does. If he is a master thief, which we must admit he is, then he would not have one plan for getting away. He'd have ten. One would be a secondary disguise, like a simple mustache. If that failed, which it, of course, would have under the circumstances, falling from a great height, he would surely have a tertiary one to throw us off. He could turn a corner, rip off his sweater and be just a man with a mustache and a tattoo, and take off the mustache and the false tattoo when some of us double back looking for him. So, let us not bother looking for a man with those distinguishing features."

Oy vey, Zaporavo thought. "What then?"

"His eyes. I have them frozen in my mind and will never

forget them. No matter what beard or Groucho Marx nose and glasses he puts on, I will recognize those eyes.

"So, let us look at every man in a hotel or hostel, since we all know the trains and airport are being searched, and the roads've been blocked since yesterday, and he had to hide somewhere."

"Wait," Zaporavo said. "Why's this been happening?"

George remembered that the Dreadnaughts only just arrived, on the private Hentzau jet from God-knows-where. From their secret cave under the sea where they slept until the evil family called upon them, he thought.

"Because of the robbery," he said.

"What robbery?"

"The museum was robbed of a painting shortly before we were. The city is trying to keep it hush-hush and avoid scandal before the big art opening tonight."

"Really."

"Mm-hmmm."

"Let me guess. The museum is owned by Hentzau, so it therefore has all the finest security in the world, just like this building, and it comes as a shock that it has been breached."

"…Yes."

"Just like this building."

"Yep."

Every eye looking at Sansoucy narrowed, and he suddenly wished that he was far, far away from that conference room.

X

When Trevor and Danny limped into Stubble's house they were greeted with disgust. The three men who did not stink of skunk shouted for them to get out and not let the door hit 'im in the boongie. It was the same welcome they'd received from everyone they had met along the way.

The hotel staff had no interest in having them arrested; no one wanted them to be detained anywhere near them until the police could arrive, so they were not only free to go, they were keenly encouraged to.

Now they were determined to be let into the apartment they'd designated as the hideout and official place for hostage storage, and they'd be damned if they would be spoken to that way, after the misadventure they'd had. In the line of duty, no less.

Stubble, whose name was Jock—he had been named Jacques, but didn't think it sounded masculine enough, so he'd changed it, while also adopting a working-class British accent—wouldn't allow them in and didn't care how they'd come to be that way.

"You go back to yer own flats an git woshed up! Y'ain't comin in here, not on me life!"

"Ar flats're clear cross town! We'll never make it, not wiffout the fuzz pickin us up!" Trevor snapped.

"Ain't no copper in the world would arrest you lot! He'd have to have no nose to suffer that stench. You got a free pass to Timbuktu. You can go anywhere in the world you like, and no punter'll stop ye."

"Well, yer the punter who's tryin. Gang way and lemme at yer bath."

"I said clear off!"

"Who got outta bed at two in the mornin' to come nab

yer poof? Who came runnin' to help you out in the dead of night? I was comfortably off in dreamy dreamland, I was! I was snugglin up to that bird Nigella what makes them fancy dishes on the telly, but I roused meself and came quick, fast, and in a hurry to do yeh bidding. And this is the thanks I get."

"My back's haff broke," Danny said. "An it's on yer head. A bit a 'ospitality is wot I'm afta."

"But ye *stink,* so ye do!" Jock shouted.

"Aye," said the other two in unison.

"Was that other one ye sent us to get, ambushed us in the loo. Put chimneys on us both, he did, then popped a wee stink bomb or summat. Phew, it's awful. There was no call for that. You think yer sufferin, Jockie boy? You dunno the haff of it, limpin' ar way here cos no one'd let us in their cab."

"That's right," Trevor went on. "An' we did it fer *you.* So I say a bit a gratitude is in order."

Jock screwed up his bristly face and looked at them for a moment out of one eye, then sighed heavily.

"Git in the bathtub," he said reluctantly, jerking a thumb over his shoulder. "An' don't you leave a ring around it when you get out."

Trevor shouldered his way past Danny. "Me first."

"Like hell!" Danny said.

The two of them began a shoving match, which turned into a fistfight. Jock and the other two tried to shout them into a truce, but none of them wanted to actually touch them to pull them apart, so things began to get knocked over and broken.

Lex, who sat tied to a chair in the middle of the room with his scarf on as a blindfold, shook his head at them.

Zaporavo went up to the archives with George to speak to the woman who'd seen the ghost, and she showed them where she had felt its presence the strongest. She felt silly talking to them about it, but was relieved that they took her seriously. When she pointed out the area where she was convinced it had been, she still got the chills. She remembered that there'd been a small green light that did not belong...right...here. Here by the USB port. So it must have been a flash drive, copying some file or other. The light disappeared, which must have been the invisible man disconnecting it, but she was too busy having a small heart attack to think at the time. Now it was obvious.

Zaporavo went to that section of the aisle and took deep breaths through his nose. George watched him a moment, in a mixture of distaste and fear, wondering if he was trying to find their prey's scent, like a dog. Like a heavily-tattooed bloodhound.

"And what might've been copied?" George asked the woman.

"Oh, there are all kinds of files there. *Forbidden files,* of course."

He frowned at the subtext in her voice, and met her eyes. She was trying to tell him something with her eyes, a telepathic message, and for a moment he was confused.

"Files that," she went on. "If made public, could bring this entire empire crashing down. A *lot* of indictments, you, me—"

One of the rules of working for the Hentzaus was that you never ask questions. Everyone knew that they were taking part in something...not necessarily legal. But it was a job and there were benefits. Other companies would eventually go under for one reason or another, but none of the Hentzaus' ever did. It was stable work. If one kept his head down, hands in his pockets, and mouth shut there was no reason to worry.

Now that some file—*any* file—was out there it could mean curtains for the family and definitely for him.

George began to think of his own mortality, and how he'd really rather live a long and happy life. That thought has made many millions of people throughout the history of the world a bit desperate at one time or another. It has made them willing to do things they would not normally do. Like get themselves some kind of insurance.

His thoughts must've been plain to read as they crossed his face, because the woman seemed satisfied enough to slip a flash drive into his hand. Their eyes met again, and this time there was no misunderstanding.

Zaporavo followed the thread of scent he had picked up down the aisle away from them, and the woman whispered "If we're to find which file was copied, you probably ought to see what would be of interest, yes?" Then, she stepped away from him and said in her normal voice, "This area is restricted, so I will have to accompany you back to the elevator, sir."

Zaporavo called out "The stairs!" and the woman made an either-or tilting of her head and said "Or the stairs."

Sansoucy followed Zaporavo following his nose, down the stairs, along the corridor on the ground floor to the front door and outside. The Dreadnaughts had noticed them and stopped whatever they were doing to come after them.

"Which way?" the mercenary asked gruffly. The wind was too strong and too many people had been in and out since the thief had escaped to pick up the trail again.

Sansoucy pointed, and they went across the street, down the sidewalk to the corner, then out across the boardwalk to the wrought-iron railing. The head of security pointed at the bench where they'd taken the lanyard and the bungee cord for fingerprinting and a few other tests, and they leaned over the railing to look at the grass of the park beneath.

"Where do I get down?" Zaporavo asked.

George shook his head. "There is a bridge over there that we can cross and get to the stairs on the other side. Our thief chose his escape well."

The mercenary looked at the other Dreadnaughts and with no more than a jerk of his head, told them 'Let's go.' One of them had a coil of black rope over one shoulder, which he let drop to hang from his wrist. One of the others took an end of it over to a nearby tree and deftly tied a double overhand knot. Some of the men put on gloves, but Zaporavo didn't, and he looked critically at George, knowing the man in black was now feeling uncomfortable, and loving it. His malevolent eyes said 'You probably won't follow us,' and George clenched his jaw.

The mercenary took the coil of rope from the extended arm of his colleague, and flung it over the wrought-iron railing into the clear blue of the sky, where it spun and unfurled and fell to swing beneath them. Grabbing the thick braid, he vaulted over the rail and disappeared.

Startled, in spite of himself, George rushed to the railing and watched in disbelief as the man slid down the rope all the way to the bottom. The other Dreadnaughts laughed, then one by one they shouldered him aside and followed their leader. If they could do it, George thought, he could, but he didn't want to try. Not this way, at least, with no safety belt, or a net below him, or even gloves. But those terrible men were far beneath him now, looking up with contempt in their eyes.

He had to do it, or look like a coward—which, he reasoned, shouldn't matter, since he didn't care one bit what *these* men thought of him. They were trash. They were scum who killed for a living. What could their opinions possibly mean to him? But still, he felt the burn of their eyes and knew he had to do it, or he'd remember this day with shame for the rest of his life.

As he grabbed the rope with his suddenly wet and slippery hands, he wondered which makes someone the bigger coward, to not do a stupid thing he knows is dangerous and unnecessary, or go ahead and do it because he is afraid of what others will think of him. As he swung his leg over the railing, knowing he had officially gone too far, and hating himself for it, he knew it was the latter. It takes a different kind of bravery to do the smart thing and not follow the rest of the idiots.

He swallowed hard and swung his other leg over the railing, thinking 'It really isn't too late. I can say to Hell with them right now and go back to my office. That's where I should be, anyway. What am I even *doing* out here?'

He leaned way out with only his toes on the boardwalk, an unnerving emptiness behind his back, and a sobering certainty that the rope could snap at any minute. For some reason, the flash drive in his pocket felt very heavy. *He* felt very heavy.

He closed his eyes, held his breath, and down he went.

His tension made him swing, and trying to stop swinging made him swing even more, but he just kept his eyes shut and put one hand under the other under the other under the other until his desperately reaching feet touched the ground. With a gasp of relief, he sagged onto the grass and opened his eyes, a part of him expecting the others to laugh and cheer and maybe pat him on the back or ruffle his hair, but they didn't. They all just looked down at him with the same sneering contempt as before.

Zaporavo turned away, found the indentations in the grass where Guy had fallen, scanned the ground near them, and off he went, following something only he could see.

XI

Guy would have loved to go back to his room and get some sleep, but he knew he should change hotels before any of the employees asked him about the events the night before. Luckily for him, the top priority of the hotel's staff had been to get that awful smell out of the bathroom in the bar as quickly as possible. They would remember him soon enough, though.

He told Valentina that they should wait to receive the call from the kidnappers before contacting the police, since it took a full day before Lex could be considered missing, unless there was evidence of violence or suspicious absence.

He felt confident that he could get Lex out of harm's way in time for the art exhibition later that evening, even though he had no plan whatsoever. He knew where the hideout was, at least on the map, if not in real life, and he was Guy Fox. That alone was enough to get the job done.

Mostly, he had to do it because it was the right thing to do but, he had to admit, part of it was because he needed to be a hero to this damsel in distress. She would very soon be out of his life forever, and so he only had this short time to act, and he had better make the most of it.

When his captors had all quieted down, Lex said "It's skunk."

The five of them looked at him, and then at each other.

"Wot he say?" Jock asked.

"I said, it's skunk. What you smell like. And what you need to wash it off is tomato juice."

They all looked at one another some more, wondering wot kind a cheek he had to talk to 'em. The truth was, he had quite the delicate nose, and if he was going to be tied to a chair, he'd prefer to be as comfortable as he could until it was over. He'd had about as much as he could stand of that smell.

"Go on down to the store and buy up all the tomato juice you can find, pour it in the bath, and scrub yourselves with it."

"Here, wot you know about that?"

"There are skunks where I grew up, so I've smelt it before and I know how to get it off. Well, peroxide and baking soda is the best, but tomato juice will do the trick. Google it."

"Wot's yer game, eh, poof? Tryin' to git us all to poison arselves in the bath tub so's you can waltz roight on outta here?"

Lex sighed heavily.

"I'm sorry, boys, I really can't make out what you're saying with those ridiculous accents. Like maybe if I wasn't wearing a *blindfold* I could read the subtitles printed across the bottom of the screen here."

"Wot's he on about?" Trevor asked nobody in particular.

"Look, if I inhale anymore of that smell I'll asphyxiate and die, and then I'll be no good to you at all. Who'll pay my ransom if I'm dead? Come on, boys. Go get yourselves some of that Blood Mary mix and some vodka while you're at it, and I can be happy, you can be happy, everything'll be daisies and bunnies and hugs."

They looked at one another again, this time uncertainly.

Lex waited, patiently on the outside.

Eventually, Jock asked "So where do they sell tom*ah*-oh juice?"

They expected Lex to cough up all the money, but he pointed out that they'd nabbed him coming out of a hotel bar, where a man can drink for hours without his wallet. He had left all his money up in the room and signed a slip of paper for his tab.

Oh.

So, they all had to pool their resources, which didn't amount to much, since they were all out of work and had blown more than they'd intended in the way-too-expensive hotel bar. None wanted to ring the women in their lives to ask for a loan, since they had already borrowed as much as they could've. Besides, their women had begun to get all hoity-toity about supporting them, and the romance probably wouldn't last too much longer. They'd ask questions, too, no doubt. Best to leave them out of it.

Lex listened to them sit on the floor, since their card table had recently been broken, and put all their wadded-up notes and spare change in a pile in the middle of them. It was even a bit entertaining to hear them count and recount until they all agreed on what the total was.

Eventually they admitted it was a meager sum but it *was* an investment, and would be well worth it. They started to spend the ransom in their minds, talking about what they'd do with it and where they'd take their women to eat, what pretty things they'd buy for their old mums. Lex knew it wasn't a good time to tell them they would have to wait until his paintings sold—*if* they sold—in the show that might not even open without him. They would not take that too well, and would probably vent their frustration on him.

They still hadn't asked him whom they should call with the ransom demand. He wondered if they'd sit around waiting all day for the money to magically appear.

Guy was about to tell Valentina in the ormolu and marble lobby that he wanted to change hotels, when he glanced through the glass revolving door. He blinked in surprise at Zaporavo coming up to push his way in, and the sandy-haired man in black, and the other Dreadnaughts following in their wake. The sandy-haired man pointed at him.

"Oh," he said, locking eyes with the man in black.

Valentina raised her eyebrows at the look on his face, and followed his gaze, asking "What?"

"Trouble."

Zaporavo hadn't smelled him yet, but he saw a man looking straight at him with a the-jig-is-up look on his face, and he knew without having to ask that this was his prey. He snarled, whipping a wicked blade out of his sleeve and charging Guy.

The thief thrust Valentina behind him and leaped boldly to meet the attack. Zaporavo had expected to feint with the knife and strike with his other fist to stun his prey, and then Guy would be overwhelmed by the sheer weight of the others. They could then drag him out of the hotel with little drama, a quick smash-and-grab. But Guy somehow knew that the knife was for show, and when it came forward he leaped, his knees pistoning up to flying-snap-kick the fist that came in from the other side. His heel hit the man's knuckles with all his weight, and the shock of it jarred Zaporavo's arm from his wrist to his shoulder. He landed, putting all his momentum into a blow at the mercenary's jaw that knocked the man out cold.

The Dreadnaughts who saw it as they pushed through the revolving doors, froze, and the other section of door hit them from behind, making them fall over and block it from moving. No one had ever knocked Zaporavo out before, and the sight was enough to stun three of the men who'd seen it. The other one was George, and he allowed himself a smug little grin, but only for an instant.

He was trapped in the revolving door and could only glare at his prey, who met his gaze squarely.

Valentina grabbed Guy by the wrist and tried to pull him away.

"Vamos!" she hissed. "Let's go!"

He didn't want to run. He wanted to nip this right in the bud by beating them all, and he knew he had the chance. *And* he didn't want this poor woman to run with him and be seen as his ally by his enemies, because she really wasn't. He was an unknown cause of all her problems, and she was just mistaken about him, at least until he undid what he had done. He didn't want anyone punishing her for being on his side.

But George Sansoucy's eyes were burning into his, and he now saw Valentina, and the thief knew he had to take her with him to keep her safe.

Guy winked at George, backed up a few steps, and took Valentina's hand as he turned to run. The rush of adrenaline in his limbs made his knees shake, which the others took to mean he was afraid, but that was far from the truth.

He wished he could have a chance to get all of his toys and the painting out of his room, but they would be trapped in the hotel if they didn't run out of the back door at that very moment. He led her by the hand, tingling all over more from her fingers curled into his than by the threat of death. They ran from the marble lobby down a corridor, following the escape route he had memorized, just in case this had happened. On the way, he scooped a glass flower vase into the crook of his arm and carried it with them.

She frowned at him, wondering what he was planning to do with it. It was large, with white calla lilies, and the inside was full of iridescent pebbles to add weight and hold the flowers in place.

Valentina took her oversized Jackie Onassis sunglasses off of where they perched in her hair and held them in her free hand while they ran, grateful she was wearing sandals instead of heels. She hoped Guy knew where he was going.

She replayed the last few moments in her mind again and again as they ran, the feeling of him pushing her behind him protectively, the sight of him leaping to meet that ugly, horrible man, the surprise of watching him win so quickly and decisively. And the *zing!* of electricity that passed from his hand when they turned to run and his fingers curled into hers. The excitement of running away with him, her feeling complete trust that no matter what happened, she was safe at his side.

They rounded a corner, and Guy let go of Valentina's hand to grab the stems of the lilies, yanking them out of the vase as he poured the contents out all over the marble floor. The iridescent little vase gems clattered and bounced away, spreading out behind them, and they ran to a door marked Service Entrance. Guy turned in midstep to hit the push bar with his hip and bounce it open, ushering her through it first and looking back the way they came. Around the corner came the Dreadnaughts, running at full tilt. The forerunners' feet landed on the pebbles on the floor and down they went, sprawling face-first onto the cold marble, tripping the men coming behind them comically over them.

Guy went through the door, reached into a rhododendron bush nearby that grew next to a small tree, and pulled out the hooked end of his spare bungee cord. He'd tied it around the tree trunk after the fight last night, just in case he'd have to make a getaway later. Stretching it, he hooked it onto the door's handle, locking it from outside.

He handed Valentina the flowers and smiled. She snorted a quick laugh, and then they ran for all they were worth.

XII

Amanda Hentzau stepped out of a candy-apple red '75 Midget convertible and bumped the door shut with her hip, her Burberry mini skirt tight around her bottom. Later that day, she would go to the art exhibition looking for a new artsy hipster boy toy with which to annoy Daddy, but for now, she needed coffee.

Her last boyfriend thought it was funny that she cared way too much about the provenance of her coffee, with all the scrutiny of a wine snob, but would throw down any old thing when it came to drinking at the club. The fact that he had said that was the reason he was her *last* boyfriend.

She would only drink coffee in a trendy little place called Higher Grounds, because their coffee came from an organic peasant co-op on the Volcan de Agua in Guatemala that used no slave labor, and had succeeded in spite of the contradictory Free Trade Agreement. At least, that's what the hipster barista had told her. It was really from right there in Ruritania, and it was as organic as plastic. But she would sip it and look up thoughtfully, contemplating the flavor, and say things like 'Bursting with vibrance, full-bodied with silky texture,' and other nonsense.

She came around the front of her little car and stepped up onto the curb, but shrank back just in time as two people ran past her, the fabric of a woman's cream cardigan grazing her forearm. She huffed at the outrage of it, almost being knocked over in the street by common trolls. Why, she could have been pushed out into the road and run over!

She could've been killed!

The time spent in recovery from her shock alone was an atrocity, because it kept her from her coffee and her peace of mind. She didn't understand why Daddy didn't just kill the lot of them, just nuke them all and get it over with.

She clomped down the sidewalk in her platform shoes toward the coffee shop, glancing at her reflection in the window of every parked car she passed.

"Do you think they're behind us?" Valentina asked.

"Probably."

"You don't think we've run far enough?"

"I don't know if the *moon* is far enough."

"Well, let me catch my breath."

They slowed to a stop and she bent to put her hands on her knees and gasp. Guy didn't seem fazed. He kept an eye out behind them, then checked their surroundings.

"I love that place," he said, pointing at a sign on a restaurant across the street. It said Riposte. "We went because I'm really into fencing, and they have swords on all of the walls."

"Fencing?" she asked.

"Sword fighting."

"Really?" She stood up straight. "Is the food any good?"

"Are you kidding? It's excellent."

"Then let's go in. I haven't had breakfast yet."

"Oh, wow, I forgot. You must be starving."

The restaurant was done mostly in ivory and burnt umber, their version of black and white. All the furniture was blond wood that had been painted white, and then sanded to let a lot of the wood grain show through and look rustic. Then epees and French poetry in cursive had been stenciled onto them in black. There were real swords on the exposed brick walls here and there, and hanging ferns that gave an occasional splash of color.

The music was electro swing—old jazz like Louis Prima or Ella Fitzgerald remixed with modern beats. At that moment, the Andrews Sisters were singing a funky version of "Rum & Coca-Cola" that made Guy nostalgic.

He indicated the sign with a jerk of his chin.

"The name means, in fencing, when you parry, or block an attack, and then counterattack. I think, but I'm not sure, that it means the dishes are their answer to tradition. Other people have been making these meals for centuries, and these fusions are their rebuttal."

"What do you mean?"

"Madam, m'sieur," a condescending maitre d' said, bowing ever so slightly from behind his podium.

"Deux, s'il vous plaît," Guy said, holding up two fingers.

"Sorry?"

"Two, please."

"Oh."

Guy stifled a laugh at the pompous man pretending to be French, who couldn't understand even that much.

They followed him to a table next to the noisy kitchen and Guy said "We'll have a better table, if you please."

"I'm sorry," the man said, with his nose in the air. "That is quite impossible."

Considering the escape they'd just made, on top of all the tension of the morning, they were a little high-strung, and less willing to let some things slide. This man would make all that tension come to a head.

"I am not above causing a scene," Valentina told him, even though she was. The man snorted derisively.

Guy made a show of being discreet, taking a folded twenty euro note out of his pocket, palming it, and slipped it to the man in a handshake. It was one of the counterfeit bills he had on hand to give to rude people who expected to be bribed. It looked real enough at a glance, but whenever they tried to spend it somewhere, they'd at least be embarrassed, and at most, arrested.

"Oh look," the maitre d' said. "A better table just became available. Right this way, please."

He led them down an aisle with black framed pen-and-ink sketched portraits of all the great masters—Bonetti, Thibeault, Fabris, Sainct, Agrippa and Capo Ferro. Swords hung with naked blades on the walls between them.

"You should not have done that," Valentina said to him in Spanish, leaning into his shoulder as they followed. Guy's lips grew thin in a smug little grin. He changed the subject.

"One of the things I like about this place," he said. "When you buy some of the really good bread or pastries to take with you, they wrap it up in parchment that is printed with French poetry written in script. It is reminiscent of *Cyrano de Bergerac*. You ever see that?"

"Hum a few bars."

"A play written in 1897. Big-nosed dueling French soldier? With a gift of words and a tragically unrequited love? No?"

She shook her head while the maitre d' stood beside their new table and conspicuously did not pull out her chair. Guy pulled it out for her instead, and she curtsied.

"Merci," she said.

"Avec plaisir."

The maitre d' gave them both leather-bound menus, and bowed with an embarrassingly insincere graciousness before leaving.

"Anyway," Guy went on. "In Act II, the hero goes to the bakery of his friend Ragueneau, who's recently been bitten by the poetry bug. His wife is mad at him because they have their business to run and instead he's sitting there writing poetry, so she takes his poems and uses them to wrap pastries. I think that's what it is supposed to be when they do it here."

"That's a nice touch," she said, grateful for something else to talk about than their adventure.

"I wonder if it's true, or I just assumed all of that."

"Either way, I like it. So, what's good here?"

She opened the menu and frowned at it.

"It's a fusion place," he said. "They've got a really good Indian version of ratatouille, with an orange reduction and cardamom and a bunch of other spices. Everything except curry, I think. The lamb bourguignon is really good, too. It's got cardamom, saffron, cumin, and something else, I can't remember."

"Are you a chef or something? How you know all of the ingredients? It doesn't say on the menu."

He shrugged, pretending it was nothing, feigning humility. "What do you want to drink?" he asked.

She flipped to the Drinks page and frowned. "Cosmo?"

He snorted.

"What?"

"Have you ever had a cosmo?"

"Well, no." Then, she laughed. "I have a friend in Guate who has a restaurant, and whenever he interviews waiters, he asks them what cocktails they can make. You wouldn't believe how many say *'whiskey en las rocas,' 'vodka en las rocas,' 'ron en las rocas.'*"

"You're kidding."

"I wish I was. But we're getting better. There are a lot of good bartenders and chefs, now."

"Okay, but if you're going to have a cocktail, don't have a cosmo. That was a drink the fun-loving, independent ladies on *Sex and the City* made trendy, but it was still twenty years ago."

"Snob."

"Oh, you dunno the half of it."

"Well, go on, then. Tell me what I should have, then. *A mojito?*"

"God, no."

"Ha! Why not?"

"That drink is a bartender's worst nightmare. It takes five minutes to make, and he'll be sitting there muddling the mint leaves and thinking up ways to poison you the whole time."

"Long Island Iced Tea?"

"Only college kids drink that. Or men trying to look cool in long-sleeved shirts that advertize fake surf shops."

"Really?"

"Yeah, they wear their hats backwards to show they are still kids at heart."

She laughed again, the tension disappearing, and she wanted him to keep going. "Gin and tonic?"

"That's for people who wear their polo shirts with the collar up, and have unimaginative tattoos to show they're somewhat edgy. Usually tribal, or unverified Chinese characters."

"Oh, I know. They'll pick symbols that they *think* mean 'strength' or 'courage,' but really mean 'peanut butter,' or 'Tuesday.' Okay, so what's next?"

"Whiskey and ginger ale. That is for people who want others to see them drinking whiskey, but they don't really want to have to drink it. They also want to appear to play sports, so they'll saturate their Wall with photos of their coed company softball games. They will probably pop their collar, too."

"So what do *you* drink?"

"Raspberry Jell-o shots."

"Hm, I don't see it on the menu."

"Me neither."

"I'll have a Coke, then."

"Good choice. What you want to eat?"

"I dunno. What's good?"

"Well, they do a fusion of French and Indian cuisines, like that Indian version of ratatouille I told you about. That is really good. Roasted bell peppers, eggplant, zucchini, capers and olives, and the sauce is a reduced orange juice with cardamom and saffron, and all kinds of stuff, really. It's good. And they have lamb bourguignon, an Indian version with cardamom, cinnamon, everything but curry. I think it's because if anyone was going to do a fusion of French and Indian food, they'd just make a French dish and put curry in it, so the chef here purposely avoided using curry. I like that. He second-guessed the semi-innovative."

"What?"

"Never mind."

"What are you going to have?"

"The croque madame."

She scanned the menu for it and, finding it, read aloud.

"Ciabatta bread with gruyére melted on top, mozzarella melted inside, tomato, ham, mushrooms and…garlic confit? What's that?"

"I don't know yet," he said, smiling quietly.

"You don't *know?* How do you not *know?"* she teased.

"I don't know *yet.*"

"Mmm, look at you, all confident. So, you're going to have that, and what, it has an egg on top?"

"Yeah, a fried egg. They pour this creamy sauce all over it, and then put the egg, and when you pierce the yolk with your fork, the goo mixes with the sauce and it's *so* good."

"I don't believe you."

"You don't?"

"No. I demand proof."

"I'll let you have some, then."

"Just a bite."

At that moment, the maitre d' looked up in alarm and tried to step in the way of George and the Dreadnaughts, asking if they'd had a reservation as they strode into the restaurant, but the man in black pushed him aside.

"Just remembered something," Valentina said, closing her menu. "Before we came in here, you said We. We came here because they have swords on the wall. Who's 'we'?"

Oops, Guy thought.

Game over.

The moment has finally arrived. The moment I have been dreading, when I have to tell her I am married and break the spell. He steeled himself and looked up to meet her eyes.

Just as hers looked over his shoulder and widened.

Zaporavo's lips curled cruelly as he came around the corner with the others, and he saw their prey. He was taken aback by the look on the man's face, though. When Guy pushed his chair back and stood to meet them, he didn't seem afraid at all. He seemed *relieved,* as if their presence was welcome and right in the nick of time. To this man, the threat of the Dreadnaughts ranked down there with the fine for an overdue library book.

The lack of fear on his face stung Zaporavo's pride.

Guy Fox reached to take a sword from the wall, a rapier, a boyish smile baring his dazzling white teeth. He sliced the air a few times with it as they approached, getting a feel for the weight.

Valentina shrank back in her seat, the terrified look on her face more befitting the occasion.

"We're trapped!" she cried.

Guy turned and winked at her. "Never."

When Sansoucy saw Guy with his sword at the ready, he snatched another rapier off of the wall, and shouldered Zaporavo aside. He was delighted to have an opportunity to show off his skills in front of all the men who'd recently put him down, and with a smug tone he said to the mercenary, "This is *my* bag."

Zaporavo scowled, and would have killed George just on general principle, but decided to let their fugitive tire himself out by killing him, instead. His fist and jaw still hurt from earlier, much as he hated to admit it.

George assumed the stance, his eyes burning into Guy's.

Guy smiled again, composed himself, and said "Hallo. My name is Inigo Montoya. You keeled my fadda. *Prepare to die.*"

There was a pause, nobody else quite believing he'd said that, especially George. People who had been eating before the killers walked in, who had only a moment before been frightened, now began to giggle at their tables.

George blinked. This man took *nothing* seriously at all! He'd stolen the moment and made him look like a fool!

His lips grew thin and tight, and he touched his blade to Guy's in a silvery, ringing glissade that made the world hold its breath. Like sprung steel mousetraps, they snapped forward and wove a shimmering web of steel between them, the blades clashing furiously. Strokes like lightning were met with impossibly deft parries, and countered. Cunning feints and shrewd lunges were performed with a speed that defied reason. Their slender, wickedly delicate blades were flashes of light that dazzled the eyes of the spectators.

Back and forth they went, up and down the aisles, hampered by tables and chairs, taking care not to hurt the people sitting beside them, and that made the fighting all the more difficult. There was no freedom to use the methods of the masters on the walls.

People had taken out their camera phones and were now recording it, watching the fight on the screens instead of with their own eyes, and grinning like voyeurs. Valentina sat frozen in her seat, her knuckles white as she gripped the tablecloth.

George was good. Almost constant practice had given him speed and strength that made all the Dreadnaughts, and even Zaporavo, grunt in appreciation. He was cold too, and without fear. A Zen-like smile curved his lips, unnerving to see. At least, unnerving to all except Guy.

The look of childlike joy on the thief's face made the diners think this was a show for their entertainment, but it angered George no end. It made him start fighting to prove something instead of just to win. He had to teach this impudent fool a lesson, and that would be his undoing.

He began to lunge prematurely, and too often, recovering a little too late and with less dignity.

It became clear before too long that Guy was better.

Not by much, but enough. In many small ways, he was the better swordsman, a split second faster, a hair stronger.

And that damnable smile. It shook George to see it.

The din of their battle was like the clashing of cymbals in the restaurant, punctuating the upbeat jazz, and the spectators on both sides watched breathlessly, until—

From a low parry, Guy's point seemed to be everywhere at once, dazzling George and making him panic, and then with a tight, deft circle, he wrapped his blade around the other and flipped it up and out of Sansoucy's hand. From the salon came a collective gasp, and Guy lunged.

George's stricken face went white as he felt the point stick in his breastbone, saw the blade bend between them, saw the leer in Guy's face as he leaned in and held his gaze. For a tense moment, the tableau held, the thief making sure George knew he'd been beaten before winking and skipping back two steps.

With snarls of rage, the Dreadnaughts pulled out ninja throwing stars and tiny knives from what seemed like thin air, and hurled them at Guy in a terrifying barrage of flashing steel. All the diners squealed and ducked this time and only George saw the flashing web of steel that Guy wove before him. He stood there and blinked, unbelieving, as sparks flashed all around the thief. Ninja stars and throwing knives thunked into the walls and the furniture across the room, sometimes mere inches away from some innocent bystander's wide eyes. But not one touched him.

Guy's cool had finally broken; his eyes blazed with rage.

An instant that seemed like an eternity later, the last of the throwing knives was batted away with a *tink!* and it clattered on the floor somewhere. For a moment, there was no sound except the heavy breathing of the men in the room.

Guy was exhausted. He had had no sleep and more than enough excitement, and now was spent. There was nothing he could do now but bluff, and so he put the most threatening look he could muster into his cold eyes, while Valentina came up behind him. She had dug her pepper spray out of her purse and now stuck her arm across his heaving shoulder to spray an X at their attackers.

The brown spray billowed out and stung George and the Dreadnaughts, and the diners at their tables, but hey, it happens. They could have moved earlier. She felt no pity for them as she dragged Guy away.

He turned and stumbled along the aisle toward the restaurant's side door, passing tables behind which people still crouched, peering around the tablecloths and warily holding their camera phones up like periscopes.

On a far wall, a throwing knife that hadn't lodged very deeply slipped out and clattered on the floor.

XIII

When Jock and his gang had finally gotten enough cash together, after digging through dirty clothes on the floor in the corner of the bedroom, and looking under the couch cushions, they left the two stinkers behind to watch Lex. The other three happily went to go buy tomato juice and get away from the horrible smell.

They still had not thought to ring the hotel and notify anyone that Lex had been kidnapped, to demand a ransom. Their hostage wondered if he should do them the favor of reminding them, because that would certainly speed up the process, but he decided it best to keep his mouth shut.

After a while of listening to the two men grumbling, he cleared his throat. They looked over at him.

"Um…listen, I'm awful hungry," he said.

Trevor and Danny looked at each other.

"I know, you probably don't care, but I haven't eaten in what feels like days, and I don't think I'll last much longer. Really, I won't be much use to you as a hostage if I die. I mean, who'll want to pay for me, you know? It's totally in your interest to keep me alive."

They rolled their eyes, and Trevor said "I'll whip you up some gruel when I get around to it."

"Gruel? I don't even know what that is! Seriously, I have a very discriminating palate, and I could go into anaphylactic shock if you give me the wrong thing. I have a tricky tummy, too," he added. "Really, that's the price you pay for only ever drinking expensive wine. No, I think if you could braise me a duck breast or something, that'd be lovely."

"One bowl of gruel coming right up."

"No! What did I just tell you?"

"You'll be lucky if Jock even *has* gruel in here," Danny

muttered. "He's not one to keep much in his larder."

"Well, would you mind looking?"

The two kidnappers looked at the floor, grumbled a bit more, then reluctantly got up to look in cabinets, really only to shut Lex up. They banged around for a moment, making noise to satisfy him that they were indeed looking, but soon they noticed that they were pretty hungry themselves. They had been up all night, after all, and walked a long way after losing a fight. On cue, their stomachs growled.

"There's bugger all here," Danny said sadly. "Just some bread and a little spices wot was here when he moved in."

"Spices?" Lex asked, perking up. "Which spices?"

The thug scowled over his shoulder at their hostage.

"I dunno!" he growled. "Spices!"

"Yes, but it makes a world of difference. What does it say on the little labels?"

"*Grrr.* Um…nutmeg."

Lex made that down-curving smile and nodded.

"Um…cardamom?"

"Cardamom, yes, that's good. What else?"

"Saffron…"

"Here, tell you what, could you take this blindfold off? It'd be a lot easier if I could see."

"Nope. We gotta leave it on. You're a 'ostage after all."

"Yeah, but I can at least spot something. Then you can put it back on."

They looked at each other again, silently debating it for a bit with facial expressions, before agreeing that it wouldn't do any harm. Trevor limped over and untied the scarf, and Lex blinked and made wide-eyed faces, making a show of adjusting his eyes to the light.

"Wow, so *bright* in here." It wasn't, but so what? "Okay, now, where are we? Ah, there you are. Okay, can you hold a few of those things up? I…hmmm, I tell you what. Do you think you could scoot my chair a little closer to the cabinet so I could see?"

"You can see fine from there."

"Not really. My eyes are tired from being blindfolded."

"Well…"

"Ooh, is that sherry?"

"What?"

"That bottle, it looks like cooking sherry. If it is, you can get one of those frying pans and sauté some garlic and onions in oil, whatever oil there is, I mean there's got to be oil *some*where in this house, right? Sauté it and put a splash of that sherry in there, maybe some cream? And then cook that bread in it. It'll be *so* good. You'll love it.

"Wot, just that? Bread?"

"You'd be surprised."

They grudgingly followed his directions, not happy at all about how finely he wanted the garlic minced, or how strict he was about the temperature of the oil. At one point, they decided to purposely defy him and put the garlic and onion into the pan when he had told them not to, and it sizzled into charred little lumps immediately.

"Hey! You burned it! I said the oil was too hot and you needed to let it cool down a little!"

"You and your oil!" Danny snapped. "I ought splash it in yer smug little face!"

"Well, we won't get breakfast that way, now, will we?"

"It's not like we're *chefs*, here!"

"Sheesh. Here, let me do it," Lex said, as if to children.

"Yeah, *you* do it!"

They untied him and folded their arms expectantly, like sullen teenagers, while he poured the ruined oil in the sink and washed the pan. Then, he gave them a course on the proper way to handle a knife as he minced another clove of garlic. They watched him with feigned indifference, trying not to show first their curiosity, then their actual interest.

"Now, we start over with the oil," Lex said, putting the pan back on the burner. "You have to *watch* it, or else you burn the onions, like we just saw. Now, who wants to try and cut the onion like I just did? Come on, don't be shy."

Hentzau asked the man in charge of background checks at the Illuminati headquarters in Zenda who this thief could be, and was told it would be a few minutes. He hung up the phone and tapped his pen against his pursed lips while he thought. After a moment, he leaned forward and picked up the phone again, dialing his secretary.

"Yes, Count?" she asked.

"Daphne, get in here."

"Yes, Count." She hung up and opened the door, coming into his office, her red high heels click-clicking on the marble floor, her eyebrows raised in a facial "What?"

"Daphne, what is directly under my desk?"

"Um, on the floor beneath us?"

"Yes."

"I believe it is the women's executive rest room, sir."

"Well, I want you to look into putting a tank there."

"A *tank*, sir?"

"Like an aquarium. You know, for fish."

"Where the women's bathroom is?"

"Yes."

"You mean, taking out the women's bathroom?"

"Yes."

"To put a fish tank in?"

"Yes. Well, no. A shark tank."

"Okay."

"And I want you to see about having a button-operated trap door installed, up here in my office."

She looked at him a second, then nodded.

"Anything else, Count?"

"That'll be all for now."

She nodded, turned on her heel, and click-clicked back out of the office, wondering if he would notice the trapdoor being installed directly under his chair.

Valentina hailed a taxi, one of the old-fashioned green and cream '48 Chevy checker cabs that prowled the streets, and ushered Guy into it, casting wary looks about her before getting in after him.

"Anywhere, just drive," she said.

The cab driver turned in his seat to look over the rim of his sunglasses at her.

"Really?" he said. "They say that in movies when the hero is being chased."

"Just go, please."

"Are you being chased?"

"No."

"You are, aren't you?"

"Okay, yes, we are."

"It costs more if you're being chased, just so you know. Because of the element of danger."

"We're not being chased, then."

"You sure?"

"Positive. Just go."

"Where to?"

"Just drive!"

"Sheesh. You're American, aren't you?"

They pulled away from the curb and into a shoal of cars.

George left the Dreadnaughts to run around town doing whatever they wanted, and he meant to drag his wounded pride and his burning eyes back to headquarters. After the morning he had, he wanted to just sit down and relax, and if he got ambitious later, ask the librarian what she'd meant.

Right now, though, just a quiet cup of coffee.

He passed Higher Grounds, stopped, and remembered something his chef ex-boyfriend had said once. Capsaicin, the chemical in peppers that makes them hot, is fat soluble, so drinking water makes it worse. Casein, a protein in milk, binds to capsaicin, neutralizing the burn. The chef would control the heat of peppers by using them in milk-based sauces, and people could enjoy the flavor without having to suffer for it.

The Dreadnaughts were back there splashing water in their faces to get the pepper spray off, and making it worse, spreading the burn to their hands and getting it even more in their eyes than it already had been. George saw that and, blinking his red eyes, he'd staggered outside and down the street, saw a sign advertizing a latte special, and a light bulb went on over his head.

Had his companions thought of this, they would have just barged into the coffee shop, looked for the milk, and snatched it out of an employee's hand, splashing it in their faces in front of God and everybody. But George, however, was a gentleman. Even with his face in searing pain, he kept calm and went to the counter, waiting his turn and politely asking for a glass of milk.

"A latte? How big?" the hipster barista asked.

"Not a latte. A glass of milk. Just milk, please."

"Um, we don't serve just milk."

"It would mean a lot if you did. I can't tell you how much it would mean to me."

The young man looked at George's scarlet face, and the tears glistening on his burned cheeks.

"Coming right up."

"You're too kind."

He waited patiently for his glass, said "Thank you," and turned with it towards the men's room. At that moment, Amanda Hentzau came out of the ladies' with her fuchsia Louis Vuitton hanging from the crook of her arm, and her fuchsia iPhone10 held up in front of her. She was daintily swiping right on Tinder with the pinkie of her other hand, and clomping along in her platform shoes, when she walked straight into George, splashing milk up out of his glass and onto his sleeve.

"Omi*god!* Watch where you're going, you jerk!"

George heaved a sigh, not recognizing her because he could not see as well as he would have liked, and she didn't look at him long enough to recognize him. Most likely because he wasn't wearing a mirror. It's just as well. If she *had* recognized him, he'd be lucky just getting fired.

He got to the men's room and hunched over the sink, dipping his cupped fingers into the milk and wiping his eyes with it. It took a moment, but a blessed coolness soothed the burning in his eyes. He gasped in relief, and breathed a silent "Thank you, God!" as he started splashing his face.

The door opened, and he heard someone come in, stop, and stare at him for a moment, but he really didn't care how he looked or what someone thought of him. He was full of joy that his idea had worked, and at the discovery that the greatest pleasure is the relief of pain.

"Jean Francois," he mumbled. "You arrogant bastard, you just saved my life."

Valentina cradled Guy's head in her lap as the taxi went off to wherever it was going. His heart was racing too much for him to fall asleep, but he was so weak he melted into the back seat, and the warmth of her. She gazed down at his handsome face, and began to trace it lovingly with the tips of her fingers. Here was a real man, she thought.

"You know," she said. "Futuro, I know of a prophecy you could fulfill."

George ordered a coffee and sagged onto a stool at the counter. For a moment, he was still, but then he noticed in the corner of his eye that the coffee shop was also an internet café with desktop computers along one wall.

Remembering the USB in his pocket, he asked the barista if he could use one. The young man nodded, gestured with a wide sweep of his hand and said "Whichever's free."

Sansoucy took his coffee over to one of them, fished the small flash drive out of his pocket, where it got momentarily tangled up with his keys, tried to plug it in, cursed and turned it over so it would fit, plugged it in correctly, and waited for it to go *doot!* His security-trained ears were picking up all the chatter of coffee shop patrons around him, subconsciously sifting through it for any hints of danger, until he saw the names of files on the drive. Then, for him, all was silence.

XIV

On September 11, 2001, the attacks on the World Trade Center and the Pentagon were orchestrated by the Hentzau family with the complicity of Britain and the United States, as a pretext for removing the liberty of people worldwide in exchange for security. They used the attacks to gain control of the few nations in the world who don't allow Hentzau central banks, such as Afghanistan, which was attacked by US forces less than one month afterward.

Physics professor Stephen E. Jones of Brigham Young University published a paper in which he proves the World Trade Center buildings could have only been brought down in the manner they were by explosives.

He received no coverage in the mainstream media—the Hentzau-owned mainstream media—but the evidence can be seen online.

It was revealed that, prior to the attack, millions of dollars of options on both American and United Airlines were traded by Hentzau agents. Following the attack, anonymous letters containing anthrax were sent to various politicians and media executives. Like the 9/11 attack, this was immediately blamed on Al-Qaeda, until it was discovered that the anthrax contained within those letters is a specific type of weaponized anthrax made by a US military laboratory.

Two years into an investigation of AIPAC's (The American Israel Public Affairs Committee—the largest political lobbying group in the US with over 65,000 members) possible role as a spy front for Israel, Larry Franklin, mid-level Pentagon Analyst, was observed in 2004 by the FBI giving classified information to two officials of AIPAC who had been suspected of being Hentzau spies.

AIPAC hired lawyer Nathan Lewin to handle their legal

defense, the same lawyer who defended suspected Hentzau spy Stephen Bryen in 1978. Larry Franklin worked in the Pentagon Office of Special Plans, run by Richard Perle. At the time, Perle—who was caught giving classified information to Israel back in 1970—was insisting that Iraq was crawling with weapons of mass destruction, calling for the US invasion.

There were no weapons of mass destruction, of course, and Perle has dumped the blame for the "bad intelligence" on George Tenet. With *at least* two suspected Hentzau spies inside the office from which the lies that launched the war in Iraq originated, it appears that the people of the United States are the victims of a colossal deadly hoax.

The leaking of the investigation of AIPAC to the media on August 28th 2004 gave advance warning to other spies working with Franklin. The damage to the FBI's investigation was completed when US Attorney General John Ashcroft ordered the FBI to stop all arrests in the case.

On July 7th 2005, the London Underground Network was bombed. Israel's Finance Minister, Binyamin Netanyahu was in London on the morning of the attacks. He was there to attend an economic conference in a hotel over the underground station where one of the blasts occurred, but stayed in his hotel room instead after he had been informed by Israeli intelligence officials attacks were expected. These and other terrorist attacks were blamed on Muslims, to justify continued war in the Middle East. The Hentzau-owned news media bombarded the West with stories of atrocities committed by Muslim men against their women, and all of the bad guys in action movies were Muslim terrorists since the 1990s, to make the people in Audienceland believe that Islam is a religion of evil and hate, turning the world against them. Popular opinion in the US became "nuke 'em all."

Anyone who says anything about this is now automatically branded a "conspiracy theorist," a negative term that puts a sane, reasonable person in the same category as those people who wear hats made of aluminum foil to keep the government from reading their thoughts. They are laughed at and then dismissed. That association is the work of the Hentzaus, to discredit those who dare to question them. As the poet Baudelaire once said, the greatest trick the Devil ever pulled was convincing the world he didn't exist.

There are now only five nations left in the world without a Hentzau-controlled central bank: Iran, North Korea, Sudan, Cuba, and Libya. Recent news implies that will soon change for all five countries, in one way or another.

George sat back in his chair, stunned.

Roughly four thousand miles away, in Langley, Virginia, a man trying to grow a mustache hung up the phone at his desk, turned in his chair, and said to another "Remember Guy Fox?"

The other man, with longish hair, frowned, then opened his eyes wide. The first man nodded.

"Yeah. Guy…"

The man with longish hair asked "What about him?"

"Well, apparently he broke into ol' Rupert Hentzau's office building and copied some files."

"You're kidding."

The first man shook his head.

"Well, what's he trying to do? Who's he working for?"

"No idea. Yet."

"Whatever he's up to, he's in over his head."

"You think so?"

"You *don't?*"

"I dunno. You never know with Guy."

"Hm. That's true."

"Hentzau's people just called me to ask who their thief could've been. I didn't tell them it was obviously Guy. But I'll have to tell them something."

"Whatcha goan do?"

The first man shrugged. "Ask the Director, I guess."

"He'll definitely want us to go over there and apprehend him. Try to get the suit back, at least."

"I could do with a quick trip over there. Get out of here for a few days."

"Then it's settled. We have hard evidence that it's him, and we know exactly where he is. Who knows? We might run into him in a bar somewhere, if he still drinks."

The first man swiveled around in his chair and picked the phone back up, dialing the Director's office.

The apartment door flew open, and Jock and the other two thugs came in with one can of tomato juice, shouting about the hell of a day they'd had, and froze in their tracks. Lex Cargo sat at the old wire spool that Jock had been using as his end table with Trevor and Danny, sopping up sauce with bread and chatting like they were old friends.

The three thugs stared, speechless, at the other three, who looked up at them as if they were crazy.

"Wot?" Trevor asked.

XV

"We can't go back to our hotel," Guy said.

"But why not? We'll just explain to the police…"

"I…" Guy started, but there was nothing he could say. "And enough of this. We have to report José missing."

"José? Who is José?"

"My brother! Oh, right. You know him as Lex."

"That isn't his name? Lex Cargo?"

"Hahaha, no, it's not. We don't know where he came up with that name. Well, the Lex is from his middle name, that is obvious enough. Alejandro. He is José Alejandro Morales and I'm Maria Valentina Morales. But he needed to have an artist's name, so he picked that one. Lex Cargo."

"It works."

She made a yes-no tilting of her head.

"In our family, we always called him Chepe."

"Really? Why?"

"That's what you call people named José. Like Francisco is Paco, or Roberto is Choby. Or Futuro is *guapo*."

Guy was so tired he almost didn't catch that, but when it registered in his head, he looked at her in surprise. She was smiling at him with adoring eyes, and she gently bit her lower lip, waiting for him to lean in and kiss her. He felt his cheeks flame scarlet, and he knew this was it.

He bit the bullet and blurted it out.

"I'm married, Val."

The light went out of her eyes, her smile faded, and it was the most heartbreaking thing he thought he'd ever see.

"I'm sorry." He had never felt as stupid as he did saying that. "I really am."

She swallowed hard, looked away. Cleared her throat.

"So…"

Guy felt her pull away from him even though she stayed put on the backseat of the cab. He felt the drawbridge of her castle being raised, and he hated himself for allowing this to have happened in the first place.

"So," she said, rallying herself. "Where's your wife?"

"Far away."

She looked at him again. "How far?"

"Very far."

The faintest glimmer reappeared in those eyes, trying to salvage something. Maybe they were separated. Maybe—

"So, she'll never know."

"*I* will know."

She set her jaw and smiled bitterly. Turned to look out the window at trees flashing by, and the clouds.

George dragged and dropped copies of every file on the USB onto the computer's desktop, putting them in a new file entitled "Top Secret." He knew if he had called it "Must Read" no one would look at it, but if it was secret, everyone and their dog would click on it.

It's like when someone says "Don't look behind you," the first thing you'll do is whip around and spoil whatever they are trying to keep secret, but if they say "Look behind you, right now" you'll narrow your eyes and go "Whyyyy?"

So, he left the Top Secret files there for all the world to see, and went back to Hentzau headquarters to hand in his resignation.

"Let me out here," Valentina said to the driver.

Guy opened his mouth to speak, to stop her, but shut it again because he knew it was for the best. The only reason he had ever entertained any thoughts was because of the argument he had had the night before with his wife, but he knew in his heart that he would never cheat on her, and it was better for all concerned that this beautiful damsel in distress walk out of his life forever.

The green and cream Checker cab pulled up to the curb, and she waited a moment, looking at the back of the seat in front of her, waiting for any reason at all not to go, but one did not come. So, with a heavy heart, she clicked open the door, stepped outside, and let it softly *chunk* shut.

The breeze that gathered up the ends of her cardigan was cold, and she hugged herself as she watched the cab pull away. She watched the rear window to see if he would turn to look at her through it, but the dark shadow of his head never moved.

Inside, he held up dentist's mirror-on-a-stick to watch her without her knowing, and his heart sank.

As George walked back to the office building, he began to think about the man he had chased, and fought, and lost to that day. They'd pursued him for infiltrating the offices and copying a file, or many. Now that he had seen the files that may have been of interest, he could understand a thief wanting them, and realized that he might not be a bad guy.

Especially since, until he tendered his resignation, *he* was one of the bad guys. Which made this thief a good guy, to some extent. Of course, George had a hard time not hating the man for defeating him back there in the restaurant. But it was a hate tempered with grudging respect.

So, George didn't know exactly where he stood at the moment. It was difficult.

The city of Zenda was partly old and partly new, with a fair amount of ancient Baroque buildings and narrow tree-lined streets, contrasting with wide modern boulevards and spacious residential areas. The modern additions to the city had been modeled somewhat after pre-war France, in the hopes of recreating what had been lost.

Valentina did not marvel at the beauty of the city as she walked listlessly in her gold sandals. She stared with sad eyes that saw nothing.

The tragedy of the situation had finally engulfed her. If the distraction of danger and the thrill of excitement with Guy had kept the truth from hitting her before, now that he was gone it was suffocating her. Lex was gone. Snatched up by some evil thing that hid in the darkness and sent its little demons to torment her, to chase her all over the city. There was nowhere she could go to be safe from them, and now that she had embarrassed herself, and fled the cab to escape her shame, she had lost the one ally she had.

And she'd left her purse with all her money and credit cards in her room at the hotel.

At that moment, an encrypted call from a remote castle in Switzerland, that loomed forbiddingly, perched atop a pine-covered mountain with its spires wreathed in wisps of cloud, bounced off of a satellite and was relayed to Guy's smartphone in Zenda.

He looked at the screen, listening to the ringtone, for a long moment, until it rang out.

The man who was trying to grow a mustache—a brown one—was Calvin Maguire, Guy's old friend from that night in the restaurant in Virginia, the night that the mystery girl swept in and captured the hearts of everyone who saw her. Maguire thought for a moment, trying to remember her name, and couldn't. He went to a filing cabinet, pulled open a drawer, and finger-danced through the files there until he came to Guy's. Pulling it out, he propped it open against the cabinet and rapidly scanned each page until he found it. The AWOL report. The night that Guy had slipped out of a high security facility that there was no escaping, just slipped out as if he were a ghost, and went to meet Sharon Dorothy Grace and make out with her under the stars.

That was what put him on probation. Then, creating and then somehow launching his own satellite into space so he could write "Sharon, will you marry me?" in the sky, using Agency resources, was the last straw. They canned him like a tuna. The day he left, however, the invisibility suit he had made, also using Agency resources, mysteriously disappeared. Both Guy and Sharon dropped off the face of the Earth, and he became a bit of a legend around the office.

If something inexplicable happened, somewhere in the world, they said "Guy did it." He was the go-to explanation.

"Hey, did you hear? The Hope Diamond reappeared in Brussels, and then disappeared again."

"Must've been Guy."

"King Tut's tomb was stolen from New York's Museum of Natural History!"

"Guy took it."

"The Mona Lisa is gone, too!"

"Guy Fox, no doubt about it."

But this time, Maguire knew in his heart that it *was* Guy, and he knew he was going down for it. This would be the last chance to get that suit back for the Agency.

Or, Maguire thought, get that suit for himself.

The man with the longish hair was Chris Hammond, the one who had started the Guy-did-it joke, and his specialty was hacking into computers and cellular phone lines. He'd come up with a port flooder, which sends a million requests per second to every port on a server, which couldn't possibly handle all of that at one time, so the overload crashes the server. *Kaboom.*

He also invented a port blocker. If a modem worked on a phone line, there was a safety default that would automatically disconnect it if the phone was picked up, but there is still a slim chance of someone hearing you. So, he was using a cable modem. With a cable modem, you can spy on somebody and never get caught. Ever.

What it does, it keeps the modem port open so you can go in and turn everything on, disabling the LED light so they won't have any idea it's on. You can turn on the mic, the camera, the speakers, everything, and use their webcam to look at them, use their microphone to hear them, and talk to them through their speakers. He used to love to terrify other people with it, especially on April Fool's Day.

Hammond had been the one to help Guy with the satellite, and he had surreptitiously installed a way to listen in on signals bounced off of it. He had not used it in a while, but now took his red cell phone out of a small lead box where he kept it under his desk. He'd made it red because of the phone Commissioner Gordon used to call Batman.

While Maguire was off in the room with the filing cabinets, Hammond called Guy's satellite.

The second time Guy's phone rang, he frowned at the screen. It was an unknown number. Who in the *world* could call him on that phone without him knowing? Warily, he answered it, looking out the window of the cab at the sky.

"Why, hallo, Meester Bond," a spooky voice said.

XVI

Count Rupert of Hentzau was changing clothes to go to the art exhibition by that Guatemalan guy at his museum, not because he liked the man's art, but because he wanted to see what was so good that someone would go to all the trouble of infiltrating the place and stealing a painting.

While pulling on his military-style jacket, he paused. He frowned for a moment at his reflection, then reached down to push a button on the phone on his desk.

"Daphne?"

"Yes, Count?"

"Did you see about the shark tank?"

Pause.

"Um, I'm working on that right now, Count."

"Good. Daphne?"

"Yes, Count?"

"I'm thinking crocodiles, instead."

Pause.

"Very good, sir."

"That is all."

"Yes sir."

Hentzau pulled his jacket the rest of the way on and began to fasten the buttons, whistling "My Blue Heaven."

"Who's this?" Guy asked.

"Never mind that. Why are you still in Zenda?"

"What makes you think I'm in Zenda?"

"I *know* you are in Zenda, Futuro. And I know what you've done."

"No, you don't."

"Yes. I do."

"I haven't done anything."

"Yes, you have."

"Nope. And I'm not in Zenda."

"You are, too. I'm looking at you right now with your satellite."

"Impossible. I don't have a satellite."

The spooky voice sighed.

"It's me, Guy. Chris."

"Chris?"

"Chris Hammond."

"Chris Hammond?"

"Yeah."

"Oh, hey. How you been?"

"I'm all right."

"That's good. How's the wife?"

"I never married."

"That's good, too. So, what's up?"

"Aw, nuthin'. Aside from you being in grave danger."

"Oh yeah?"

"And how. Listen, you've got to get out of there. Zenda is closing in around you. The airport, the train station, every road out of there. And forget the police, the Dreadnaughts are looking for you."

"Oh, is that who those guys were?"

"Don't be cocky, Futuro," Hammond warned.

"Cocky, lazy, dead," they said in unison, their old rule.

"I know," Guy muttered, as if to a nagging parent.

"So, have you fulfilled any prophecies, yet?"

"Hmph! Not yet."

"Remember that one we made up, all those years ago?"

Guy thought of Val and smiled. "Hum a few bars?"

"That you'd save the world."

"Oh, yeah. That one. You know that prophecies are just vague assurances made up by optimistic oppressed people to give groundless hope to other, more gullible oppressed people, right?"

"Who you working for?"

"Nobody."

"Fine, don't tell me. Just listen, time is running out. Why haven't you gotten out of there yet?"

Guy was quiet for a moment, and then admitted "There is something I have to do."

"What?"

"This guy got kidnapped, and it's my fault."

"Not your problem. Your problem is you."

"Not this time."

"Why not?"

"I have to do the right thing."

"Oh, listen to you," Hammond teased. "I have to do the right thing! Since when do you care about the right thing?"

"Today." His voice had the finality of a driven nail.

Hammond knew it was useless trying to argue with him. "Okay. Just so you know, we're coming to get you."

Guy laughed, thinking it would be nice to see his old friends again.

"Catch me if you can," he said.

Valentina decided that, since she had no way of getting back to her hotel because she had no idea where she was, and no means of paying her transportation, and with her inherent distrust of the police that came from her upbringing, that she had no options but to go to the art exhibition and try to talk to somebody there.

She stared up at a banner advertizing the show, hanging on the side of a grey Baroque building, that said it was only a few blocks away, and she took its advice.

Guy hung up the phone, and his brain began to whir. If those people chasing him had no means of finding him, he was sure they would assume Valentina could be tortured to give up his location, which she wouldn't know either. They would assume that she wasn't talking because she loved him and would never give him up, so they would hurt her even worse, make her suffer even more, until she died. He could not allow it.

He thought briefly on the type of people who tortured. From his stint in the CIA, he had come to learn that power and torture are similar, in that they are their own end. The Hentzaus, for example, did not take control of the world so they could make it a better place. They took control so they could *be* in control. Torturers do not get into the business of torturing to extract information from people who don't want to give it, to help a government make the world safer or pave the way for democracy. They do it just because they really want to hurt somebody, and getting hired to do it is the only way to do it and get away with it. Or better, get *paid* for it. And they don't want it to be over with too quickly, so they are happy when someone is tough and doesn't give in.

He had always been prepared for the day when he'd be tied to a chair in a dark room with one swinging light bulb. He knew it would come as surely as he knew he would one day die, and so he had taken steps to make sure those two days would never be the same.

Now that he had to delay his escape even more, his eyes grew hard, steeling himself for what was to come.

Hammond and Maguire stood in front of the Director's desk, their right hands holding their left wrists in front of them, blocking their crotches. That last part was what occurred to the Director at the moment, and made him grunt a short laugh. *Why do people do that?* he asked himself.

"You're sure it's him?" he asked.

Maguire nodded solemnly. "Positive."

"But why do we have to get involved? Let Old Man Hentzau bring in his Dreadnaughts to take care of it.

"Well," Maguire said, taking out his smartphone and tapping the screen with his thumb. "There's this."

He handed the phone across the desk to the Director, who tilted his face upwards to peer down his nose at it through his small glasses. It was a YouTube video taken an hour or so earlier with another smartphone, four thousand miles away. My, the things we can do these days, the Director thought, grunting again.

Hammond and Maguire stood there for several minutes, holding their wrists and listening to the tinny sounds of the recorded clash of blades.

"That's him, all right," the Director said. He made more grunts of approval from time to time, until the climax when Guy defied all reason. The two men listening glanced at one another, remembering the sight, and raised their eyebrows and nodded in co-appreciation of it.

When the last *clink!* was heard, the Director's mouth was hanging open. The video lasted a moment longer, got shaky and made him dizzy, and ended. He made a down-curving, tight-lipped smile and nodded.

"That's our boy."

"And those were the invincible Dreadnaughts," Maguire chimed in. "Getting vinced."

"But the video doesn't show him getting away."

"Oh, he got away," Hammond said.

"How do you know?"

Hammond bit his tongue. He couldn't very well say he'd just talked to him. Just *happened* to have his number and call him up a few minutes ago.

Maguire kept their momentum going and distracted the Director. "But time is running out, and we have this one chance to get over there and grab him before it's too late. I really don't think Guy will stick his neck out like this again, not after being recorded on YouTube. I mean, this thing is going viral already. My guess is, if he gets away this time, we'll never hear from him again."

"So? We've got bigger fish to fry than him."

"Sir," he said, letting go of his wrist to put his knuckles on the desk, for emphasis. "If he *does* get caught, and by the Dreadnaughts, of all people, they'll have that suit he made."

The Director's eyes widened. Maguire nodded.

"Yes. *Our* suit."

The Director pounded his fist on the heavily-doodled blotter of his desk.

"Over my dead body!"

Maguire cut his eyes slyly back at Hammond, who made a face of *Careful.* Don't let him see you.

Guy thought about all of the things that could, and probably *would* go wrong, and planned accordingly. If this happened, he'd do this. If that happened, he'd do that. He ended up with ten plans, one for every likely contingency, and a few others just for the hell of it.

Then, he went back to the hotel. He couldn't just waltz right in through the front door without having to answer a lot of embarrassing questions, so he went around the building to where, thankfully, his other spare bungee cord was still stretched taut from the sill of his room's open window, tied to the trunk of a tree. Luckily, no one who worked for the hotel had seen it, wondered about it, and untied it.

He looked around to make sure no one was looking, ready to kick rocks and whistle casually if anyone was, saw that he was unobserved, and wrapped the cord around one arm. Taking out his knife with the other hand, he slashed it in one blow, rocketing himself up the side of the building and onto the ledge, sitting. With a deft swivel of his hips, he was inside his room again, where all his disguises and little gadgets were.

Two hours later, he was at the train station, looking at a photo of himself on a wanted poster, grateful that he had so many disguises to wear. He watched the ever-vigilant police that were scrutinizing people's documents and searching all their bags, and was also grateful he had left the painting in his hotel room.

For a moment, he hesitated. He knew without a doubt that he could get through the security checkpoints. Once on that train, though, that was it. He'd be home free, but Lex would still be a hostage and Valentina would still be at risk.

He thought about Christ in the garden of Gethsemane, considering his options. He knew what he had to do, but he sure didn't want to do it. And of course, in the end, he had done it, and thank God he did, right? But man, he still got crucified. And Guy knew, what with all he'd done in his life, he wasn't about to ascend anywhere.

He heaved a sigh, rented a locker, and stashed his bags in it, hoping he'd have a chance to come back and get them.

XVII

Zaporavo, for all he knew, was left as an infant on the doorstep of a Shaolin monastery. That is where his memory began, and he had no reason to doubt it. He grew up there with his brothers, the other orphans left there, to become the Dreadnaughts. He had been told that he was born on a battlefield, and the first sounds he heard were the shots that killed his parents. He'd no reason to doubt it, so it was the truth.

The monks taught them their ways of discipline and of violence from the moment they were old enough to make a fist, and they grew up hard, suckled at the teats of war. They were periodically sent out into the jungle, naked and alone, and were expected to return after three days and not before. Those that survived were welcomed with great honor and allowed to rest for a whole day before resuming their training. Those that did not were very rare.

One of the exercises they practiced was the dodging of bullets. A monk would aim a pistol at them from twenty paces away, and they were to judge the path of the bullets fired by watching the barrel. If it was aimed directly at them they had to anticipate which side the shooter favored, and dodge in the other direction. The rounds were all blanks, but the boys didn't know that, so it didn't matter. It instilled in them a faith in themselves and a conviction that nothing could kill them. That made them the most fearsome enemies when they were eventually adopted by their new masters, the dreaded Hentzaus.

They had the fierce loyalty of dogs, and would do the bidding of their new masters without question.

George wondered what their reaction would be to the file he had found on them.

Guy remembered his wife, back when she was still just a girl he was sneaking out to see, asking if he was a Democrat or a Republican. He said "neither," and she said "Libertarian, then?" He shook his head and smiled a cryptic smile.

"You know the WWF?" he asked.

She frowned. "That wrestling show?"

"Yeah. Who did you like better? Hulk Hogan, Macho Man Randy Savage, or the Nature Boy Rick Flair?"

"Um...I didn't ever care about any of them?"

"Why? Because you knew it was all fake, just a big soap opera of mindless entertainment that only existed to distract people from how badly they were being screwed by the upper one percent?"

She looked at him with growing concern. He went on.

"Politics is sports for people who don't watch sports. None of what candidates say will ever be implemented after they enter office, and government will never be changed, and all of this arguing is just a big smoke screen. Asking me if I am a Democrat or a Republican is like asking me which puppet I prefer, the one on the left or the one on the right. Neither. I'm afraid of the man who is holding onto both."

"And who is that man?" she asked.

Guy remembered that conversation when he came face to face with Count Rupert Hentzau at the opening of Lex's exhibition, standing there with a glass of white and a bored look on his face. There he is, he thought. The most powerful man in the world. By chance, they locked eyes across the room for a moment, and had Guy been at the top of his game, he would not have telegraphed his every thought for the man to see, but as it was, his eyes said clearly "I know who you are," and Hentzau felt like an elephant who finds himself challenged by a mouse.

Ahhh, he said to himself. Someone to crush.

He began making his way toward Guy, who turned and looked at the impressive array of hors d'oeuvres and pre-filled glasses of wine, hoping vainly that he would find a cup of coffee hidden there. Wine would only make him more tired, and he was starting to hallucinate from the lack of sleep. If he were to be found by that seemingly unshake-able posse that was chasing him, he knew in his heart that he would not survive.

He reached up to tentatively stroke his false goatee and push his glasses up on his nose, then tuck a wayward strand of hair from his wig behind his ear. It was hot in there with his invisibility suit on under his clothes, and even though he had showered back in his hotel room, he was sticky with sweat again. It didn't matter. It might be necessary, and that was justification enough.

He had not spotted Valentina yet. Part of him hoped that she would come so he could warn her to get on a plane back to Guatemala, and part of him hoped that she already had, even though he knew she would not leave without her brother. And, he had to admit, part of him wanted her to fall off of a bridge into a river or get caught in a burning building, so he could save her, and show her in a dignified manner how he felt about her, even though nothing would ever happen after that.

He noticed a young socialite in the crowd that he'd seen often in the papers and on the covers of gossip rags in the checkout line at the grocery store. She was wearing a Bur-berry *ensemble* that made her look vaguely like a St. Trinian's girl, a Catholic schoolgirl gone bad. She had a Lego Princess Leia swinging from her keychain. Guy wondered what the significance was while he watched her be fascinated with the group of hipsters that seemed to be holding a meeting nearby, conspicuously apart yet in the middle of the show.

There was a young man with a long, bushy ginger beard and a blond Crispin haircut, wearing a burgundy and black plaid shirt, short sleeved—with the sleeves rolled up—blue slacks with purple flowers, also rolled up to emphasize that he was wearing white canvas shoes with no socks, with his man purse hanging from the crook of one arm. That arm was all sleeved in tattoos, a red rose for his elbow piece, a Stuka and a Spitfire in a dogfight, koi fish, a crescent moon, a pheasant, and either an Egyptian canopic jar or a hot air balloon, it was hard to tell. And teal Turkish slippers.

Young people with various weird hairdos and clothing, and facial piercings were listening to him lecture them about hipsterism and its fading popularity in Ruritania. They stood in poses, mostly with arms folded across their chests and one hip cocked, affecting a brand of disinterest while being wholly enthralled.

"Peak beard was reached in 2014," he was saying. "Since then, it's been on the decline. The more commonplace a thing is, the less attractive it becomes, naturally, and this was especially the case with Victorian preacher style beards. I do not have this beard because I am trying to hold onto a fading style, and definitely not because I am unaware of the movement of trends, but because I am actually making an ironic rebellion. As it goes out of style, with me it becomes very In. And, for the record, it is an Assyrian beard."

A lot of people nodded sagely, the rings in their noses glinting in the lights.

Guy wondered who was keeping a record.

"So, I would not say that I am a hipster, because that doesn't mean anything anymore. It's become commercialized and therefore irrelevant. But I would not say that I am *not* a hipster. What was once an umbrella term for a coun-ter-culture tribe of young creatives like us in Williamsburg and Hackney has morphed into a pejorative term—a sub-culture that values independent thinking, counter-culture, progressive politics, *rebels* who deviate from the norm, like hippies, has now been turned into a commercial parody."

The others shook their heads at the state of the world today, and how they were a dying breed. There just weren't any young people anymore.

The non-hipster was an artist-chef with no job and no money, but that was okay because he was against being part of the proletariat anyway, and was rebelling against all that conformist work-to-survive nonsense. His audience of fel-low non-hipsters nodded their assent, and made faces of disgust at the thought of Work. It was *so* not them.

Meanwhile, and this is what bothered Guy most, not a one of them looked at the art on the walls.

They *talked* about it, sure. They recited what had been written about it in magazines and online, but none of them actually looked at it. The only reason they'd shown up is that art shows were the place to be, just because, and there stood Amanda Hentzau, one of the heiresses of the most powerful family in the world, looking for a future boyfriend among them.

Guy spotted the curator, who was standing nervously with light reflecting off of his glasses, making him look a bit like a frightened animal whose eyes glowed in the light of an oncoming car. He knew that man must be worrying about Lex and wondering when he'd show up. Poor guy. So far, no one had asked about the missing painting. He must've been waiting for someone to ask, so he could recite the lie he had rehearsed all day, and the fact that it never happened made him constantly on edge.

He then spotted Valentina, at the same moment that she turned her head and noticed him. There was a moment of confusion, when she saw his disguise and wondered who this strange man was who winked at her, and then her eyes widened.

Hentzau arrived at his side, setting down his now-empty wine glass and taking a full one, holding it by the rim with his fingertips instead of by the stem. He turned to look at the crowd with Guy, who felt uncomfortable. The thief saw him in his periphery, lifting the glass and turning his hand to cup the bowl in his palm, bringing it to his lips.

The most powerful man in the world seemed to watch the young socialite, the St. Trinian's girl, while he drank, but not with an attitude of admiration. Guy wondered who she was to him. He became more consciously aware of Count Hentzau's body guards stationed all around the gallery, all in the traditional uniform instead of plain black.

They were in beige and celeste, with epaulets and gold braided rope and tassels. Medals for some feigned distinction in military service hung in rows from colored ribbon over the left side of their chests, and the spiked lobster tail helmets on their heads reminded Guy of Prussians in World War I. Their cavalry boots were immaculately polished.

Hentzau was also in the pseudo-military outfit affected by Ruritanians in recent years. Instead of wearing tuxedos at weddings, and suits at funerals and public events like these, they were trying to revive the traditional dress. He wore a mostly cream uniform with gold braid crisscrossing his torso in an upside-down triangle, looping around gold buttons on the sides. His epaulets, filigree cuffs, and high stiff collar were also gold, and a crimson sash crossed his chest from left shoulder to right hip, with a double row of medals— and even what looked like a Blue Max glinting at his throat.

Guy was willing to bet the man had never done anything to deserve those medals.

"You seem fascinated by those young people," Hentzau said, after loudly swallowing and saying "Ahhhh."

Guy made a face of "You're kidding, right?" and said "I find it fascinating that every generation's beatniks think they have no predecessor."

"Beatniks? That's a little before your time, isn't it?"

"Well, so was Jesus, but I've heard of him."

"*Touché.* So, what do you think of the art?"

"I like it. You?"

"It's garbage."

Guy looked at him, surprised. "Why?"

Hentzau shrugged. "I don't know. I don't like it. It's as simple as that. Why do *you* like it?"

Guy thought for a moment, and decided that this man wasn't worthy of him taking time to explain it, so he said "I don't know, I just do. It's as simple as that. Who's the girl?"

"What?"

"The girl you are watching."

Hentzau stiffened, angry that this nobody had *dared* to notice his daughter, and worse, notice him being unhappy with her.

"What's your name?" Hentzau asked, thinking about slashing Guy's credit rating, erasing his identity, and sending him to a dungeon wearing an iron mask.

"Brown. Jeff Brown. And you?"

Hentzau frowned. "And what do you do?"

"Oh, I do this and that."

"Young man, you'll never get rich doing this and that."

"I'm not trying to get rich."

The Count's eyebrows jumped. "Oh? Nonsense. Everyone wants to be rich."

Guy shook his head. "I learned something today."

"*Did* you, now? Tell me, then, what you learned."

"I learned that the effect you have on others is the most valuable currency there is."

"A naïve sentiment, boy, and a false one. When you live in the real world, as I do, you learn that cold hard cash is what makes a difference, and if you don't have it, you are up the creek without a paddle."

"But of what use is all the money in the world if no one likes you?"

"Ha! People will like you, trust me."

"Who? Hangers-on? People who pretend to laugh at all your jokes because they think they'll get into your will? Who think you'll invite them on vacation to Monaco with you?"

Hentzau's face went from sneeringly contemptuous to cold and bitter. Guy knew he shouldn't provoke this powerful man any further, but he couldn't help himself.

"I believe that if you were truly horrible, the only people who would be around you are parasites and bottom-feeders, waiting to get their chance, and that they wouldn't lift a finger to help you after they'd gotten it. I believe that if the people you'd pay to harm someone else liked that other person better, they would disobey you. And I believe that a man can change in one day and become someone better."

"Are you talking about *me?*" Hentzau was furious.

"No. I only just met you. I don't know enough about you to say—"

"I *know* you don't!"

Oops.

Luckily, at that moment, Amanda Hentzau glanced over to see her father looking angrily at someone, and somehow that someone was magically transformed into a handsome prince. A poor handsome prince in danger, who had to be rescued from Daddy. She hurried toward them, and one of the faces in the crowd turned to watch her go. Valentina had seen her sudden movement out of the corner of her eye and watched as she grabbed Guy by one arm and hugged it to her, saying "Darling! *There* you are!"

Her blood ran cold, thinking there was no way that was Mrs. Fox.

George's mind was in turmoil. He knew he couldn't just quit, now that he had time to think about it. He would have to find a good reason to quit, or risk being destroyed by the vengeful people he had worked so loyally for. He wondered if he could just go back to work every day, as if he knew nothing. He wondered if he could live with himself.

He also wondered if he had made a great big mistake by leaving all of those files on the desktop of a café computer.

He knew that the Hentzaus' power is so great that even if their entire evil empire was exposed, no one would ever believe they had the power to do anything about it. But at least someone else in the world would know, and maybe they would share it. Maybe it would go viral, and someone, somewhere, would do something about it.

And maybe he'd be skinned alive before that happened.

The Count was appalled. His daughter consorting with this impudent *nobody?* This arrogant fool?

He couldn't believe his eyes. He glanced at the nearest of the guards, standing ramrod straight against the wall with his helmet strap uncomfortably tight, and gestured at Guy with a tilt of his head and a menacing look. The guard nodded, looked at the two guards on either side nearest him, and they nodded, too.

One of them took his smartphone out of his uniform

slacks along with a piece of paper, slipping away from the public eye, and called Amanda's number. She felt her own phone vibrate in her free hand and let go of Guy's arm.

"Excuse me a sec," she said, frowning at the number. She didn't recognize it. Oops. She might've given it to some guy at the club the other night and forgotten. She answered it, ducking her head down to the phone instead of raising it to her ear, and Count Rupert shook his head at her posture.

"Oui?" she asked, affecting to speak French in a cheery falsetto. Off to the side, the guard held the piece of paper in front of his phone and began to crumble it slowly.

"Sorry?" she said, putting her pinkie finger in her other ear and clomping toward the door. "I can't hear you. The reception in this place is just awful."

Clomp clomp clomp clomp clomp, and she was gone.

Count Rupert rolled his eyes, annoyed that that worked. The two other guards came up behind Guy, who looked at Valentina, trying to speak to her telepathically and tell her not to move, not to get involved.

"These men will show you out," Hentzau said coldly to his new friend, knowing that Guy knew they would do no such thing. He would be dragged to a torture chamber, and the Count would come in to gloat for a bit before the fun started, and then Guy would find out if Heaven and Hell really existed.

Guy put his hands in his pockets, turning to go, but the guards did not wait to do it civilly. They seized him and push-pulled him past the guard still crumbling paper toward the other way out, so as not to be seen by Amanda. All the guests at the exhibition watched them go in surprise, but only Valentina had seen him drop a plastic card to clatter on the cold marble floor.

She casually drifted toward it while other people mur-

mured about what could have happened, stepped on it for a while to not be obvious, and eventually knelt down to pick it up. It was the green and white key card of his hotel room.

George entered the Hentzau building, nodding to the girl behind the reception desk, and waited for the elevator. He was still trying to decide what he was going to do when he noticed Raúl sitting in one of the buttoned leather armchairs off to the side. The young Colombian looked lost, so Sansoucy went over to ask if he was all right.

"Yeth," Raúl said with a lisp that had nothing to do with Castilian Spanish. "Is just, I dunno if I'm cut out for thith kind of work."

"Because of today?"

"Well…no, that was juth the worth of it. I been feeling like thith for a while."

"Really?" George sat down in the armchair across from him, the leather squeaking loudly underneath him as he settled in, making him feel very self-conscious in the lobby. He spoke with genuine concern. "Why, what's up, kiddo?"

"Well…I think about my future, and I doan see mythelf doing thith forever, yunno?"

George nodded, eyes wide in agreement. "I…yes, I have to say I've been thinking the same thing, lately."

"Really?"

George kept nodding, eyes wide, but looking at the rug.

"I juth dunno if thees is what God has in mind for me."

"You're religious?" George asked, surprised.

Raúl nodded. "I'm Catholic."

George made a face.

"What?" the Colombian asked.

"Sorry. I don't think much of the Catholic Church."

"Why?"

"Are you kidding? All of the wars? The Crusades, the Spanish Inquisition, the auto-da-fe, burning people alive, the conquest of the Americas, all the pedophile priests—"

"Hole down," Raúl said sternly. George guessed he was saying 'Hold on.' He listened patiently. "First, about the priests, yes, there were some, but not nearly as many as you think. Yeth, some have done bad things, but that is not a problem of the Church, that is a problem of men. In the world there are men who are predators and they are evil and dress in sheep's clothing to get their prey. But the exaggeration on this is a thmear campaign by haters of the Church.

"And about those other bad things, you can't apply the modern sensitivities to medieval action. We are so different in these last sixty years than the whole of human history, and have already forgotten what the world was like. I'm not saying all those atrocities were good, I'm saying that is what *everybody* was doing. You want power, you *take* it, you kill for it. Someone threatens that power, you kill them badly and publicly to make an example. It's just the way things were done. People killed each other all the time. Thanks God we are different now. We have sympathy for other people now.

"The Church was corrupt at times, because at the top, it was a bunch of politics between Orsini and Colonna families in Italy, trying to hurt one another. That wasn't fault of the Church, that was fault of men. The good that the lower people in the Church do the world is without measure; they feed and clothe the poor, heal the sick, comfort the dy—"

The elevator finally went *ding!* and the doors opened, but instead of getting up, George just squirmed loudly in his seat for a second, and stayed put.

Then Zaporavo stepped out of the elevator with murder in his wicked eyes.

XVIII

Count Rupert of Hentzau watched Guy dragged away with a sinister smile, and then remembered his daughter. If she came back in to see her boyfriend dragged away, she'd throw a tantrum and embarrass him and everyone there, so he went looking for her to have their argument somewhere more discreet.

She was off down the hall, still talking to the crumbling noise on her phone, and he heaved a bitter sigh.

"Mandy," he said, when he got to her side. She looked up at him with an expression of longsuffering contempt.

"Yes? Don't you see I'm on the *phone?"*

"Young lady, I don't know when you're going to get it through your thick skull, but you are *this* close to finding yourself cut off from the family."

"Good!" Amanda snapped. "I'll be better off!"

"Oh, really, you think so? You think one of those losers you're always picking up will support you? You think they can even cover your phone bill? Because they damn sure won't keep you in fine clothes and lodging. There won't be any ormolu and marble in the flat you'd share with those nobodies back in there."

"I don't want any of that! I'll rough it! I'll live a *real* life and make a difference!"

"How? *With those punks?* What difference do they make? Not one of them has a future. You, on the other hand, are a Hentzau."

"So what? That doesn't even mean anything anymore."

The Count closed his eyes, raised his brows, and shook his head as if to clear it. "What?"

"The world is changing. It's all different now. And it is leaving you behind." She hung up the phone and dropped it into her purse. Hentau raised an eyebrow at her.

"Really. And where did you come up with this?"

"It's all over the internet, Dad! It's on *YouTube!* They're making documentaries about you. People are copping on."

"Let me explain something to you. Nothing is changing except for the better for us. Those people that you think are copping on, are no more in a position to overthrow us than a fish is to ride a bicycle. This is the way society is, and has always been. Every year there is a new batch of kids that think they are the only ones plugged in, and everybody but them is a sad, sorry sheep. They talk about how they are all going to change the world by growing goatees and dyeing them purple, and wearing patchouli oil and facial piercings, drinking herbal tea while writing bad poetry, smoking clove cigarettes, and getting tattoos. They are all the same, year in, year out."

She stood in an attitude of defiance, her arms folded on her chest and her feet in ballet's fourth position *croisée.* The look on her face was of a girl whose mind is made up, and the answer to everything was No.

"When they finally *do* have their day in the sun, rebelling and overthrowing their betters in a coup that *we* organize, they dance and sing and send people to the guillotine until they admit that they have made a mess of things, and then in we swoop to restore order. This is the basic fact of life. There are several strata in every society, and the cream rises to the top. We are meant to govern, and they are meant to serve, and while they whine about how all men are created equal, by their very existence they prove that to be false.

"This is the natural order of things. Without Hentzaus to work behind the scenes, there would never have been an Industrial Revolution. There would never be transportation like there is now. No airplanes, no cars, and *definitely* no '75

Midget convertibles for petulant little girls like you. There'd be no internet, and no smartphone for you to look at every second of your life. No, we would all be working on a farm in some Godforsaken place, tilling the field, or in a sweatshop. There would be so summer trips to Monaco, because there wouldn't even *be* a Monaco.

"Every revolutionary that wants to overthrow society and rebuild it more to their liking has no idea how society works! Anarchy inevitably ensues, and out of that chaos, a capable few rise up to seize control and restore order. That order that is restored is exactly like what was displaced. The same thing has happened all over the world. People have no idea how to conduct themselves, Amanda! They have to be led everywhere, dragged by the leash we fasten to the rings in their noses. Do you want to be one of them? Or do you want to do the dragging?

"Your Aunt Irma came up with the style those kids were affecting back there! She decided that Beatniks would come back, but be more fashion conscious while pretending to hold fashion in contempt. She chose that hairstyle, those clothes, the man purse, *everything!* Everybody out there, from a hipster to a cholo, is a sheep! And we are the shepherds."

The iron in her will was wavering. The Count could see she faltered in her resolve, and that was enough. The seed was planted.

"Are you sure you want to trade places with them?"

She shifted her weight from one foot to the other.

"Listen," he went on, his voice softening. "I know what you're thinking. It is the most natural thing in the world. You are twenty. Every person in the world goes through the same things as they grow up. When you're three years old, you have to tell the world everything you know. When you're ten, you laugh at everything that isn't funny. When you're fourteen, you turn into a sullen little punk. No matter how good your life is, you will hate it. And then, when you turn twenty, you rebel. You and other people your age are the only people in the world who 'get it.' Everyone just a few years older than you is clueless and cramping your style.

"And then, when you are thirty, you will look at all of the twenty-year-old rebels and say 'Man, these kids today. They don't know how good they have it, and yet they complain. If only they knew what trials and tribulations *we* had when we were that age.' I promise you, you'll say it, too. I cannot tell you how shocked I was when I first heard myself say it, after raising hell during my twenties."

She looked at him in surprise, and he nodded.

"Oh yeah. I was a hellion. But I was nothing compared to my sister."

"Aunt Irma?"

"You wouldn't believe it. But we were young, too."

She shook her head slowly, eyes wide.

The Count relaxed, knowing she'd come around.

"Miss Cargo!" the curator said, and Valentina tried not to roll her eyes, putting on a polite smile. She realized that there was far more going on than she knew, especially now that Guy had been dragged away, in disguise, of all things, and she didn't know whom to trust, so she just wanted to get out of there as quickly as possible before someone came to drag her away, too.

"Yes?"

The man looked ready to have a heart attack. He bowed his head a little and peered over his glasses at her, hissing in a stage-whisper, "Would you mind telling me where your brother is?"

She feigned a gasp. "Is he not here?"

"No! We haven't seen or heard from him all day." The hapless man began to enunciate almost every other word, in case she did not get the seriousness of the situation. "*And* he is sup*posed* to give a *speech.* So if *you* could tell *him* to get here in the next *two minutes,* that would be *great!*"

"I see. Well, I just tried calling him a moment ago, and his phone's battery might be dead. I think he might be back in the hotel, getting ready. It's his habit to be fashionably late. But I can see that it is not considered fashionable here, so if you could do me the favor of helping me get to the hotel, I can bring him back with me."

"I can have a car brought around right away."

"*Would* you?"

Going down the back stairs of the museum, Guy was just about to spring into action when the guards did the one thing he had not anticipated. The one thing he did not have a plan for.

They tazed him with a stun gun from behind, knocking him out cold.

Hentzau left the exhibition, having only been there to be seen in his museum and photographed by the paparazzi for the newspapers and magazines. He couldn't get out of there fast enough. After the day he'd had, he was looking forward to watching that jerk get tortured to death in the interrogation chamber back at the office.

Four thousand miles away, Hammond and Maguire got on the Agency's Concord jet, armed to the teeth.

XIX

"Mr. Sansoucy?" the girl behind the reception desk said.

George turned, squeaking loudly, to look at her over his shoulder with his eyebrows raised.

"We have a visitor coming in the service entrance."

That was code for "Our goons are bringing someone in through the back door to be tortured upstairs."

George and Raúl looked at each other in surprise, and at Zaporavo, who touched the knife in a sheath at his belt, and loosened it with his thumb.

Valentina's heart was in her mouth the whole way back to the hotel, grateful that she had gotten a lift there and that there would be some clue awaiting her in Guy's room, but terrified of the implications. She was no closer to knowing where her brother was, and felt even more in the dark than before. On top of that, seeing Guy in disguise at the show had her at her wit's end.

Who *was* this man at whom she'd all but thrown herself?

The driver of the car was trying to make conversation, but she ignored him the whole way, since he seemed to be hitting on her. He finally fell into a cold, sullen silence and watched her resentfully in the rear view mirror.

When they pulled up in front of the revolving entrance of the hotel, she thanked him quietly and got out.

"Hey, am I supposed to wait for you, or what?"

She knew she was being rude, but there was so much noise in her head that she hurried to the entrance without a word, throwing all of her weight into pushing the door and getting it rolling. Through the glass, she saw several men in the uniform of the hotel look up at her, and then, when it was too late to stop or turn back, noticed the policemen in the lobby waiting for her.

The momentum of the revolving door carried her inside and her dark face went pale. A balding man of the hotel's management took two steps toward her, indicating the five policemen approaching her with a sweep of his hand and a polite bow.

"Ms. Morales, these gentlemen would like to speak with you," he said.

Guy awoke in a dazzlingly white room, his hands cuffed behind his back. There was one of those mirrors that no one can decide what to call, one-way or two-way, on the wall across from him, and a table and chair in between.

"Uh-oh," he thought.

George went to the interrogation room with Zaporavo and Raúl following him, wondering who it could be. What with his new point of view, he wasn't terribly comfortable torturing an enemy of someone he knew to be evil. By very definition, any enemy of the Hentzaus must be one of the "good guys" and, in his recent reversal of moral polarity, George did not want to be a bad guy anymore.

They went into the dark chamber to look out the one-way two-way mirror at the prisoner, and frowned. None of them recognized him, so it must be someone who'd rubbed any one of the Hentzaus the wrong way and was now going to suffer for it. The two guards that had brought him in did not know who he was, either.

Zaporavo grunted and left the room, going back to do whatever he was going to do before, remembering to put murder in his eyes when he was in the hall. It was starting to give him a headache, but he felt it was necessary for his image, just in case anyone saw him.

George left the dark chamber, also, and went into the interrogation room. The prisoner lifted his head when the door opened, and glared at him from behind tortoise-shell glasses. He did not look any more than thirty.

"So," George said, coming to lift one leg to half-sit on the table, playing Good Cop. "What brings you to my dungeon?"

The prisoner smiled wryly, saying nothing.

And when he did, a corner of his mustache lifted away from his upper lip.

George stared, transfixed, at the thread of dry glue that stretched from that lip to the back of the mustache, and then at the eyes that burned into his from behind the glasses. He couldn't breathe. Just being in the room with Guy, even handcuffed, with the entire garrison of the building's security at his beck and call, Sansoucy was afraid. He felt the sore spot on his breastbone where a sword had pierced him a few hours before, and tried to swallow, but his mouth was too dry.

"How…how did they catch you?"

"They don't know that they have, yet," Guy said.

"Really?"

There was a long silence. Guy did not seem to blink.

"Where did you learn to fence like that?" George asked.

Guy shrugged. "I read a book."

"Oh?"

"Yeah. It came with the sword."

"You're a funny guy."

Another long silence, and then George remembered his duty. It occurred to him finally that he had the upper hand, here. Guy was a hostage, after all.

"Who are you working for?"

"No one. I'm in this by myself."

"Are you avenging someone?"

"No."

"So…" Then finally, Sansoucy asked the question that he really wanted to ask. "Did you try to run me through and missed, and hit my bone instead?"

Guy grunted a short laugh. "Do you really think I did?"

"No. I think you did it just to show me you were better than me. To make sure I knew it."

Guy nodded.

"Just to teach me a lesson."

Guy made that down-curving smile and yes-no tilting of his head.

"But you knew what we were going to do to you. Why didn't you kill me? Why did you let me live?"

Guy took a deep breath, ballooned his cheeks, and let it out in a long sigh. Then, "You were just doing your job."

George nodded, letting that sink in for a moment.

"That was amazing, what you did after."

Guy shrugged a little, as if it was nothing.

"Are you trying to get us? Is that why you took those files?"

"Files?"

"The files you copied from our archives."

"I only took one document."

"Why?"

"Well…I just need it, that's all."

"For blackmail?"

Guy's brow wrinkled in confusion, and it seemed genuine enough to George to satisfy him.

"Look, the torturers will be here any minute, along with the boss man. I don't have a handcuff key."

"I got that covered."

"What?"

"You were saying?"

George stared at Guy, then said "Good luck."

He got up and left.

Outside, Count Rupert of Hentzau was coming down the hall with a bop in his step, whistling a happy tune with three sour-faced men behind him. He stopped in front of George and raised his fist to count off One, Two, Three.

"I'm going to need a bottle of decent wine to wash out that bilge water I was drinking at the show. I'm going to need some engineers with a sense of humor, and I'm going to need you to rig up some kind of complicated Rube Goldberg style contraption to kill this guy with. Google it if you have to, for inspiration, but I want something spectacular, like with a marble that rolls down a chute and knocks over a hammer to hit a hot water bottle that shoots its cork into a baby's boongie, making him cry, startling a sleeping parakeet so it'll squawk and try to fly away with a string tied to its tail feathers, pulling a whatever. A cannon."

Pause.

"I'll see what I can do," George said.

"I don't want you to see what you can do! I want you to do it! Those are failure phrases you're giving me, as if the thought of *not* doing it even entered your head. I don't want to hear that the possibility of not coming through on this even exists. We clear?"

"Crystal, sir."

"Good. Now, where is this punk kid?"

Raúl came out of the dark chamber behind the one-way two-way mirror and screamed. *"He's gone!"*

At that moment, something whirred on the satellite two hundred miles above them. Gears began to spin, making a red-tipped missile turn to face the glowing blue atmosphere beneath it with a long, slow creak.

Something beeped, then clicked, and a bloom of light exploded from behind the missile as three mechanical arms let it go. With a *swooooosh!* it sped off on a wide arc toward the thin clouds and the Earth below.

Valentina did her best to explain to the men assembled that she only had the word of a man she'd just met that her brother had been abducted. He approached her at breakfast and told her a tall tale, and then they were chased through Zenda by what looked like a death-metal band. She begged their pardon for being involved in a scandalous scene earlier in the lobby, but she still didn't know what it was all about.

"And Mr. Smithee is not with you now?" they asked.

"Mr. Who?"

"Alan Smithee, your companion."

She frowned, wondering if everything Guy had told her, even the ridiculous story about his name, had been a lie.

"No," she said. "He was arrested at the museum."

"By the police?" a policeman asked.

"No, by military-looking men. In helmets."

They exchanged meaningful looks that she didn't understand. She feigned weariness, touching her forehead with the back of one hand, and sighed.

"If you don't mind, I'd like to go up to my room and take a quick shower. All of this excitement today…"

"If you'd be good enough to come right back down, afterwards..?" the balding manager asked. She nodded.

Getting up out of her chair, she crossed the marble lobby to the elevator, and they watched her go. As soon as the doors closed behind her, they watched the *fleur de lis* arrow of the antique brass dial stop at three, Guy's floor, instead of going up to six, where she belonged.

166

As one, the police bolted across the lobby and up the red-carpeted marble stairs.

Hentzau and his men threw open the door to the interrogation room and stormed in, finding what looked—to anyone who ever watched TV—like the evidence of time travel. The chair was lying on its side, and next to it, a pile of empty clothes and an opened set of handcuffs.

XX

Valentina held up the key card that said 318 and looked for Guy's room, her gold sandals not making a sound on the green paisley carpet, until she heard the thunder of racing footsteps echoing on the stairs. Then, she bolted.

Desperate to find whatever clue he had left before they did, she ran down the hall, wondering why the hell they did not put room numbers in numerical order in this country.

She dropped the slippery card twice as her hands began to sweat, and cursed, having to stop to retrieve it, and the policemen came around the corner into the hall just as she got to the room.

"Stop!" they shouted, making her drop the card again. She was shaking all over, and they were coming too fast. She bent down, picking up the card, her hand shaking so hard she could barely hold onto it, tried to slide it into the lock but couldn't get it to hold still long enough.

She shut her eyes and breathed the word *Please,* steadied herself, and shoved the card in.

And nothing happened.

Zaporavo halted, the small hairs prickling on the back of his neck, and he whirled about, snatching his knife from the sheath on his belt. But the hall was empty. His eyes narrowed wickedly, knowing that *something* was there, sneaking up on him under that flickering fluorescent lighting.

Then, he heard the shouting off in the distance, echoing through the halls. And he saw something.

Maybe it was a trick of the light, maybe something blurring his vision, maybe any number of things, but he saw the wall *bend* somehow. Saw the blank white of it move a little.

While any civilized man might doubt his senses, might

assume his mind was playing tricks on him, he knew that something was wrong, and he trusted what he saw.

The shouting grew louder, and men spilled into the corridor, running his way. He eyed them warily, wondering if they would see what he saw, or crash into it on their way to him, and he waited for them to come. They all shouted at him at once, and he understood none of them, and when they were close enough, he suddenly smelled something very familiar. It was the scent of the man they had hunted.

Startled, he backed up, trying to watch them all carefully as they came, trying to see which of them was his prey in disguise, but he didn't know any of them except the Count and the sandy-haired man, and they were coming too quickly. The smell was strong now, and he turned and began to run to keep pace with it and stay ahead of them.

People on the street stopped in their tracks and pointed at the bright light in the sky, at what looked like a comet. A comet streaking out of the sky toward their city.

Among the pile of clothes in the interrogation room, a small device with a pulsating red light began to beep, and the flashes quickened.

Valentina bared her teeth in a snarl when she realized her mistake, pulled the card back out, reversed it, and stuck it back in again. The lock inside the door clicked and she shoved it open. Slipping through, she tried to slam it, but it was one of those doors with magnetic slow-closing hinges, the kind that take forever to shut to ensure they close quietly, and she threw all her weight into her shoulder against the door to push it shut.

The policemen were almost upon her, their hands outstretched to keep the door open.

As they ran, Zaporavo heard enough of what they were shouting into radios to piece together what had happened, and suddenly, he knew. Closing his eyes, he harnessed his chi, taking control of all his senses, feeling the weight of his body as he ran and the weight of everyone around him, and knew that there was someone right beside him.

He opened his eyes and lashed out with his knife hand, hitting something that should not have been there. It was his forearm that collided with whatever it was, not the knife, but it was enough. Something appeared. *Two* somethings. A blotch here and a matching one nearby, floating in midair.

The Count and his entourage came to a screeching halt, startled by what Zaporavo seemed to have made out of thin air. The floating blotches faltered an instant, and then tried to move again, but the killer jumped sideways in a flying spin kick that made another blotch appear. A corresponding fourth blotch flickered into being a few inches away from it.

Then, it began. Zaporavo let loose a barrage of punches and kicks, apparently at nothing, and something appeared with every impact. An instant later, he seemed to be blocking, and still, more blotches appeared, and some grew longer. The men watching gasped as something appeared to be taking shape, born out of violence before their very eyes.

With every punch or kick thrown or blocked, something crunched and more shapes appeared and flickered, materializing into arms and legs of someone fighting him. It was as if he called his opponent out of some other dimension. At some point, the knife was wrenched out of his hand, and it took on a mind of its own, slashing and stabbing at him before he kicked it away to clatter and slide, ringing across the floor. A floating hand flickered and appeared where the knife had been. It balled into a fist and kept fighting.

Their strikes were so fast they dazzled the eyes of the men watching, and only George realized who it must have been, and what was happening. Every stroke blocked by Guy made tiny cameras break on his forearms, the screens on the other side registering static, and every kick he aimed that was blocked did the same on his legs. The few blows that landed on his chest and abdomen, whether serious or not, broke more cameras and screens, and the images displayed on his back scrambled. With each second, he became more and more visible, until only a chunk of his head was missing and he jumped back a pace to take a breath.

Zaporavo grinned in triumph at Guy, standing there in his suit of broken hardware and hissing wires, with sparks spitting from him. He must have turned his suit on back in the interrogation room, after picking his cuffs, and simply took off the clothes he had on over his suit. Waiting against the wall next to the door, he slipped out of the room when the men came rushing in, and would have been home free if he hadn't have sweated so much earlier.

If it weren't for *this* ugly bastard.

Guy fought to control the rage inside of him, his rage at being caught, and said coolly "You missed a spot."

Valentina couldn't get the door closed in time, and the policemen hurled themselves against it, knocking her onto the beige-carpeted floor. She cried out, and they tried not to step on her as they fell into the room.

"What are you running from?" the police shouted.

"You're chasing me!" she cried. "What did you expect?"

"What are you hiding?"

"I've told you everything!"

"Lies!"

They spread out and carefully checked inside the bathroom, the closet, and under the bed, but there was only one thing out of the ordinary for them to find.

There on the bed was a note written on hotel stationery, with a long tube on the left of it and a GPS tracking gadget on the right, on top of a map.

Zaporavo smiled, then leaped into action once more, his blows deflected less quickly and frequently, coming closer to weakening his opponent. Guy had run and fought so much in the past twenty-four hours that he had almost no stamina left, only the iron determination to endure. Where Zaporavo was fighting to win, for the sake of his pride, Guy was fighting for his life. But there is only so much a man can do. He could not risk another minute against this man.

Seeing an opening, he darted in, lifting Zaporavo's shirt and snatching out the pistol that had been wedged in the waistband of his black jeans. He skipped back two steps, thumbing the safety off, racking the slide and two-handing the gun. Zaporavo stopped, smirking and shaking his head.

"Checkmate."

Guy gasped and let his breath catch up to him, moving to get the other men in his sights as well, without having to take his aim off of the Dreadnaught. The savagery in his eyes made them all sure that he was going to fire, and they stood frozen despite years of training, waiting to die.

Zaporavo, even though he had been raised to think he could dodge bullets, knew he couldn't dodge the one that was coming, so he mustered up all the arrogance he could to mutter "I suppose you've got something clever to say."

The fire slowly left the eyes behind the broken screens and static noise, and Guy smiled. He waited a second, listening, and said "Yeah…three, two, one."

An explosion rocked the building.

The note was to Valentina. It read "I'm sorry I got you involved in this mess, and this is the best I can do to make it up to you two. If you are reading this, I am dead and can't rescue your brother like I had planned, so ask the police to help you. The X on the map (which was pretty until I got egg on it earlier) was his location this morning. If anything has changed, it may be visible on the GPS tracker. Take him this tube, please. I wish you nothing but the very best."

The policeman who read it aloud looked at Valentina. She asked "Can we go there, please?"

George, Raúl, and Zaporavo got to their feet first. The Count and his torturers were not so quick to respond, and they stayed where they had fallen for another few moments.

Guy was nowhere to be seen.

The Dreadnaught's pistol lay on the floor in several pieces, the slide having been ripped off, and the clip next to it with several rounds rolling away across the tiles. Enraged, Zaporavo raised his right foot, pulling up the cuff of his jeans and snatching out a travel-sized automatic Beretta. He took off running, the other two hot on his heels.

Rubble rained down on the parking lot, crushing a few parked cars and shattering further on the asphalt, leaving a chunk of the top floor gaping like a silent scream.

Black smoke rose and twisted in the wind of a darkening sky. No one had been in the top floor at the time, and now, all of the other floors were emptying rather quickly.

High above, another rocket howled out from the satellite and arched toward the Earth.

W

Guy cursed as he ran, furious at having all of his escape plans ruined in one fell swoop. After being knocked out in the museum, he only had four plans left, and all of them hinged on having the invisibility suit. Now he was not just visible, but *really* conspicuous, with all of that broken hardware covering his body, and a good part of his head still seemingly missing. He wasn't getting far without a change of clothes, but he had already programmed the satellite with his phone, and—Murphy's Law, and all that—reception in the building was lousy.

He couldn't stop the rockets from coming.

If everything had gone according to plan, he would have had plenty of time to get out, and so would everybody else. He was making a getaway, not trying to blow anyone up. If there were any more delays, though, he might not make it.

As if on cue, the rest of the Dreadnaughts came around the far corner, no doubt looking for their leader, and they halted in surprise. Guy sighed in annoyance, reached up to grab the network of tiny cameras and screens on his face and peel them noisily off so he could see better. They stared at his face, and then, as one, howled and charged. Knives glittered in the flickering light as they came.

Guy bared his teeth and toed his mark on the tiles like a bull, and empty-handed, sprang to meet them.

Two police cars sped down Strelsau Avenue, lights and sirens making Valentina very nervous. She always thought the cops should arrive quietly, like a thief in the night, and swoop in suddenly to knock out the bad guys and rescue a hostage without a long, drawn-out, tensions-run-high type of scenario. What she really needed was for Guy to already have been there, given the main bad guy a big sockeroo on the jaw and tangled all of his accomplices up in a net.

But that note he had left…

She tried not to think about it.

She tried to think only about her brother, whom she prayed with all her heart would be safe and sound.

George pushed himself to catch up with Zaporavo, and slapped him on the shoulder to get him to slow down.

"Zap!"

The Dreadnaught glanced at him—with murder in his eyes again—and bared his fangs. George ignored it.

"Zap! Stop a minute. Hold on!"

Reluctantly, Zaporavo slowed after they turned a corner.

"What?" he hissed.

"The man we're chasing, he's not bad."

"What're you talking about? If he is an enemy of the Count, he is as bad as they come." He said that as if he was reciting a lifelong rule, not speaking his own words.

"Your loyalty is to the Count?"

"Of course! Yours *isn't?*" he asked suspiciously.

"Listen to me. That man took a file yesterday, right?"

"Right."

"I looked at the files to see what he might have taken."

"So?"

"I saw many things. One of them was about you."

Zaporavo glared at George. There is something funny about people. Most of them don't ever want to know the truth. They would rather someone just confirm the story they are comfortable with, and if someone tries to threaten that comfort, they will fight tooth and nail and deny everything. George knew, looking into Zaporavo's eyes, that he would rather die than find out where he came from.

A voice crackled from the radio at Raúl's belt, asking if they saw the prisoner, and George glanced back at him. He was surprised to see that Raúl had a gun in his hand, held tightly in instead of fully extended like in the movies. It was pointed at the Dreadnaught's back. George's eyes widened, but he looked at Zaporavo instead.

"You were born in Morocco," he said. "Your parents are slaves at a big hashish plantation in the mountains near Chefchouane."

He gave him a moment to let that sink in.

"My prey is escaping us," Zaporavo said. But he didn't move. He didn't take another step. The anger left his eyes, but it was replaced by suspicion. "I have no parents. I was born on a battlefield."

George shook his head.

"Your great-great-great grandfather borrowed money, and because of crooked accounting and exorbitant interest rates, could never pay it back. He became a slave along with his wife and children, and grandchildren, and all of his descendants down to you and your brothers and sisters."

"My broth…" The shock of those words hit him in the face like a bucket of cold water. "My brothers are Dreadnaughts. I have no other family."

"You have sisters working in a sweatshop in Italy, making leather handbags, all day every day."

"No."

"I can prove it. All of it."

Zaporavo looked at him skeptically, but no longer with suspicion, and that was a big enough step to satisfy George.

"I was found outside of a monastery," the Dreadnaught said, reciting his story, the story he grew up with. "Life was hard. Eventually, the Count came and adopted me."

George shook his head. "The Count left you there."

Those eyes hardened again, but George continued.

"Like all of the Dreadnaughts who came before you, for almost a hundred years, you were sent to that monastery to be made into a weapon. Then, when you were ready, you all went out to strike at whoever was in your masters' way. The plantations where all your parents work, all over the world? They grow more than hash and opium. They grow people."

Zaporavo was silent for a long time. When Sansoucy felt it had been long enough, he added "And this cat we're chasing? He's apparently trying to do something about it."

Frustratingly, the Dreadnaught's eyes narrowed, as if he was sure all of this had been a lie to convince him to let the prisoner go, and he had just seen through it.

"So you're saying you *don't* want to catch him?"

"I'm saying we don't need to run quite so fast."

At that moment, they heard the echo of all the other Dreadnaughts, baying like dogs who are closing in on their prey, and Zaporavo was off down the hall to join them.

George shook his head and glanced back at Raúl, looking from his eyes down to the gun, and back again.

"And what were you up to with that?"

The Colombian shrugged. "I was goan shoot him eef he he try to do thometing. Yunno, he dint seem to like what choo said."

"You were really gonna shoot him?"

"Of course."

George smiled slowly.

"Camong, les' go!" Raúl said. "We doan wanna be late."

Zaporavo raced into the stairwell and down the checkerplated steps, around and around until he got to the floor where he had heard the screams of battle, threw open the door and stopped in his tracks. There, in the hall, lay all of his eleven brothers, some bent in impossible directions.

Guy Fox alone was standing in the middle of them, his body still flickering with static noise.

Zaporavo blinked stupidly for a moment, then snarled and raised his Beretta to fire, but out of nowhere Guy threw one of the ninja throwing stars he'd caught only a moment before. It stuck in the Dreadnaught's wrist, and Zaporavo cried out as he dropped the gun.

At that moment, another explosion rocked the building. The wall at the far end of the corridor fell away. They both tumbled over as the floor swung out from under them, and people began to slide toward the hole and the darkness beyond. Zaporavo flung his hands instinctively out in each direction, one to grab the jamb of the door he'd just left, and the other to grab a hold of the closest man to him.

It wasn't as serious as he'd thought, though. The shift was small, and nobody was falling out of the hole in the far wall. He let go and got to his feet.

Guy was struggling to rise. Apparently, he had spent the last of his strength. Zaporavo smiled triumphantly and he picked his way toward his prey, stepping over his groaning comrades. Guy noticed him coming and took a deep breath, ballooning his cheeks, trying to muster anything he had left, but by the time he rose into a crouch, his killer was standing over him. He raised his face to glare up into Zaporavo's wicked eyes, see the man's open hand with blood trickling down the palm and dripping off of his fingers. Hear the *snick!* of a pistol springing out of his sleeve, those bloody fingers closing around it.

"Checkmate," Guy muttered. Zaporavo smiled.

George and Raúl stumbled into the hall behind them, and caught their breath at the sight that met their eyes. A long moment passed. The tableau held.

"Why didn't you shoot me before?" Zaporavo asked.

"What, just now?" Guy's voice was a dry croak, like the crunch of dead leaves. Zaporavo nodded. Blood dripped from the butt of his gun to spot the floor, and Guy watched it fall in slow motion.

Everything seemed to be slowing down.

He shrugged slightly.

"You were just doing your job," he said.

Zaporavo blinked, unable to believe it.

Behind him, the radio on Raúl's belt squawked, and he listened to the Count's voice shouting "Did you get him? I want him alive, do you hear me?"

He looked at Guy's fearless eyes burning into his, and he lowered his gun.

Two shots rang out, deafening in the closeness, and he spun around ducking into a low crouch, his gun up. George was just as startled as he was, looking in surprise at Raúl, at the anemic blue smoke curling out of the barrel of his gun.

He had fired twice at the wall, and unclipped his radio from his belt. It squawked again.

"Make sure you take him alive!" the Count's voice howled.

Raúl raised the radio to his lips and held the button on the side. "He's dead."

"What?"

"Somebody just shot heem. He fell outta the building."

"Nooooo!"

"Yeth, we'll haff to go find hees body. Ees down there somewhere."

"We have to get out of this building first!" George said.

"Yeth, we gotta get out first before we all blowing up."

"Who shot him? I'll grind whoever shot him into paté!"

"I dunno who it was. It all happen so fast."

"I'll grind you up, then!"

180

"Okay."

George rolled his eyes, turned to look at Zaporavo, and his mouth dropped open. The Dreadnaught frowned at the look on the head of security's face, and looked over his own shoulder. His own mouth dropped open, too.

Guy Fox was nowhere to be seen.

Valentina wanted to come with the police, but they all insisted she stay behind in the squadcar. She didn't know why they bothered to creep up to the apartment's front door, since they'd arrived with their sirens pealing and tires screeching. She, of course, did not stay put. As soon as the cops were close enough to the door to not be able to turn around and stop her, she got out and hurried behind them, holding the tube like a baseball bat.

They heard a lot of shouting inside, and steeled themselves for whatever awaited them on the other side of that door. With pistols out, the policemen silently counted down together from Three, and one of them kicked the door in.

Storming into the small apartment, they gaped at five men standing there holding a couch, a large spool, and a rolled-up rug between them, while a flamboyant sixth man was frozen in surprise.

"What's all this, then?" one of the cops demanded.

The five thugs all looked at Lex, who said "I'm helping them makeover their apartment. Why? Who're you?"

XXII

George and Raúl helped Zaporavo drag all of the other Dreadnaughts to an elevator and pile them in, ignoring their groans of protest. They knew that elevators are death-traps during an emergency, but it was the only way to get them to the ground floor quickly. If they died on the way down, they were no worse off than if they'd been left upstairs. After they pushed the button and let the doors close, though, the three men went to the stairs and ran all the way down.

The lobby was deserted. There was no one to help them drag their injured comrades out to safety, so they did it all by themselves, making several trips. The crowd of Hentzau headquarters employees assembled in the parking lot shouted at them to get back, but they ignored them, even when they looked at the sky where the others were pointing.

Orange comets were streaking down at them out of the darkness above.

As they were helping the last Dreadnaught cross to the front door of the lobby, Count Rupert of Hentzau and his torturers came running past them, knocking George down on their way out the door. Zaporavo moved to help him stand, but Raúl was there first. Together they made it out in time and dragged each other across the parking lot to safety.

Just as the rockets smashed into the building, bursting into roiling balls of light and shattering the masonry.

One after the other exploded, shattering the tower and belching hot ash and molten rock into the night. The people screamed and pressed back out of reach of the falling rubble, watching their cars flattened in front of them.

With a long rumble and creak, the Hentzau office building sagged, hesitated a moment, and collapsed, throwing up a giant cloud of dust and smoke.

Valentina cried out, bursting through the policemen and running to her brother to throw her arms around him. He laughed in surprise, hugging her to him.

Jock and the others still stood there with the furniture in their arms, and deer-in-the-headlights looks on their faces.

"Well, you don't *look* kidnapped," the policeman said.

"What?" Lex asked. "Oh. Well, yes, I was indeed."

"Really?"

"Absolutely. They had me tied to that chair."

"But..." Jock said. "I thought we'd gotten over all that, and now we were all mates."

"Heavens, no. Take them away, officer."

"I'm so glad you're all right!" Valentina whispered.

"Uuy, I won't be if you keep squeezing!"

She laughed and let him go, her face shiny with tears.

"How did you find me?" he asked, and her face became serious. He frowned. "What is it?"

"Your friend Futuro."

"Who?"

"Futuro. Or Alan. Or whatever his name is."

"What friend?"

"He said he was with you last night. When you were... taken."

"Mmm, Tina, I don't remember much about last night. I had a lot to drink."

"You don't remember him at all? I think he'd be hard to forget." She seemed to think a moment on a deeper significance of those words.

"I remember bits and pieces, but I wouldn't know him if I saw him."

She thought about his disguise at the museum, and she

smiled bitterly. "I probably wouldn't either."

"What do you have here?" Lex asked, touching the tube she had slung by its leash over her shoulder.

"Oh! I almost forgot! He left this, telling me to bring it to you."

She pulled it off and handed it to him. He furrowed his brow and twisted off one end, looking at a rolled-up canvas inside. He pinched it with his forefinger and thumb and dragged it out, walking over to the spool to lay it down and unroll it. He gasped, recognizing it after only a glimpse, and hurriedly unfurled it.

"Bodhisattva!" Valentina cried. "How did he find it?"

But her wide eyes grew somehow even wider, and she looked up at Lex, finally understanding.

A young man with a ginger Assyrian beard, and his hair pulled up into a man-bun, dragged on an electronic cigarette at the train station. The short sleeves of his plaid button-down were rolled up to show more of the tattoos on his well-muscled arms, arms that somehow didn't match the hipster lifestyle. It was dark out, but he raised no eyebrows for wearing sunglasses as he went to open a locker and take out his luggage. All the young people were dressing like that these days.

He bobbed his head to a beat that only he seemed to hear, even though he had no headphones on.

Policemen nearby were watching him from the shadows, certain he was the man they were looking for. The men who guarded Zenda weren't flat-foots.

As he approached the ticket window, they left their ambush in the dark, moving quickly and silently toward him. When his hand pulled money out of his pocket and reached to hand it to the clerk, a thin silver bracelet snapped over his wrist, binding him to another man with a smug look on his face. He looked up in shock. The other cuff was on the man's wrist, and when the hipster tried to pull away, he felt considerable strength in the other man's arm.

The man's free hand seized the bristly ginger beard and yanked it off, startling all the policemen and halting them in midstep. Agent Maguire looked over his shoulder at them and held up his identification.

"FBI, gentlemen. Here on official business."

Hammond came out of the cafeteria with two cups of coffee and, seeing them, grinned.

"Oh good, you got him." He glanced at the policemen. "Good evening. FBI, Special Agent Cunliffe, this is Special Agent Yawmeralenski. If you could hold these for me, I can show you our paperwork."

The policemen in their snazzy blue uniforms looked at one another, and Hammond thrust his hot To Go cups into the hands of the closest one. The man blinked at him while he patted his pockets for a moment and then said "Ah!" pulling out his wallet and a folded-up warrant for the arrest of Guy Fox, Public Enemy #6. Flipping open his wallet, he showed them his FBI card, not letting them look too quickly at it, because he noticed Maguire had gotten him again, switching the photo on it for one of a monkey.

"And here's our arrest warrant," he said, shaking the folded paper open and thrusting it into another officer's hands. "If you could just sign there at the bottom we can get him on the train and off to Gitmo."

"I am afraid it doesn't work that way," an unshakeable man named Colonel Wapt said imperiously. Hammond and Maguire smiled, pulling back their unbuttoned trenchcoats to put their hands on their hips, "accidentally" showing the policemen their Kevlar vests with four holstered semiautomatic pistols on each one, and side-arms on their hips, as well. Hammond looked at the older man with his waxed, pointy white mustache.

"I'm afraid it does," he said. "If you want to scrutinize our paperwork a little better, you'll find we have crossed all the I's and dotted all the T's."

"Firearms are illegal in Zenda. We'll take those."

"You're gonna have to."

There was a long, tense silence, with most of the lower-ranking policemen wishing they'd had guns, too. The little pepper sprays on their belts and Tazers didn't inspire much confidence against those weapons.

"You'll find everything's in order," Maguire said.

Finally, Colonel Wapt's mustache bristled and he shook his head, muttering "Americans."

He reluctantly turned around and raised his hands, making a pushing gesture.

"All right, boys. They got their man, we can go now."

He cared too much about his men to risk a bloodbath, knowing that even if they managed to bring the two FBI men down in a sudden rush, most of them would die first.

Once on the train, in their private cabin, Guy sat down and wriggled his arms behind him, lifting his knees up to his chest and working his cuffed hands under his feet to bring them in front. Slipping off the plastic aglet that acted as a sheath, he revealed a handcuff key at the end of his shoe-lace. Hammond and Maguire smiled as he managed to get it into the lock, held his breath while fighting with it, and sighed when the handcuffs clicked open.

He nonchalantly handed the cuffs back to Maguire, who said "You're getting slow."

"I did it a lot quicker earlier."

"Yeah, what the hell did you get yourself into?" Hammond asked.

"Sorry. It's classified."

"Be that way. Any chance of coming back to work with us? We've been really busy lately, and it looks like we are going to have our hands full in the coming year."

"Sorry. I've developed a conscience. Besides, I'll never go back to being anyone's pawn."

"Whatever." Hammond turned to Maguire. "Thanks for switching my ID photo, jackass."

Maguire laughed. "Hey, you couldn't even pronounce my name. It's Utremelansky."

"You definitely need a better name."

"Well, it proves the photo I put isn't far off." He looked at Guy. "You know we need to take the suit."

"You're gonna have to."

A faint smile flickered at the corner of Maguire's mouth, him wanting Guy to be joking, but not sure if he was. The sudden tension in the cabin was thick enough to cut. The cabin was too small for their firearms to be of any use, and neither of the spooks wanted to fight Guy, and the quiet assurance in his voice chilled them to the bone.

Until he winked and said "Sure, you can have it."

Hammond and Maguire tried not to sigh in relief, and instead laughed it off, saying they knew he was kidding. He opened one of his suitcases and tugged out the ruined suit.

"It might've gotten banged up a little."

"My God, what the hell did you *do* to it?"

Guy grinned and shook his head, thinking about his last tangle with Zaporavo. "You wouldn't believe it."

"Okay, well, where are you off to now?"

"Sorry, that's classified, too."

"Whatever. See you round."

Guy slapped a new mustache crookedly on his upper lip

and winked again. "Yep. You probably will."

He left the cabin, going to the bathroom to change into his new disguise, and the two of them changed into their own. They did not see each other again for the rest of the trip. Guy found his own cabin, lay down on his bunk, and was fast asleep before his head hit the pillow.

George and Raúl and Zaporavo helped paramedics load the Dreadnaughts onto stretchers and then into several ambulances, that sped off into the night. Then, they reported to the Count, who was unable to speak for a long time.

Finally, he said "Before anything else happens, I'll fly with my family to Château Mouton Hentzau, my cousins' castle in France, tonight. You will accompany us," he added to Zaporavo. "And you two find that sonofabitch and whoever fired those missiles, and kill them. Nothing special, this time. Just a bullet in the head."

The three men nodded, all of them planning something very different. Hentzau nodded, too, seemed about to say something else, and then just turned on his heel and stalked off to his limousine.

Zaporavo turned to George and asked gruffly, "You're sure about what you told me?"

"I have it all here on this flash drive," the man in black said, holding up the USB. "Take it and read it, if you don't believe me."

Zaporavo sneered. "I'm not much of the reading type."

"Suit yourself."

The Dreadnaught seemed about to say something else, and then he too just stalked off without a word.

"I think I'll go home to France and see my family, too," the newly ex-head of security said, watching him go. Then he looked at Raúl. "After that…" He shrugged. "You?"

"I've never been to Franth."

"It's nice."

"I've heard. I think I'll get into the fashion scene there."

"Oh? You want to be a model?"

"Dear God, no. I'm a bit of a designer, actually."

"No kidding?"

Raúl bent his head and smiled bashfully.

"So," George said. "There's something going on behind those eyes, huh?"

They left the smoldering wreckage, and flashing lights, and chaos behind them.

At the Zenda International Airport, all of the Ruritanian Hentzaus climbed the staircase out on the apron up to their long black jet, with its especially dastardly-looking crimson H. A cold night wind howled and whipped the hair of the women, making them squint and pull their coats tighter.

None of them nodded to Odile, who smiled brightly at them anyway and welcomed them aboard. It was beneath them to acknowledge anyone in their service unless it was absolutely necessary. She was used to it, though.

At least, until Zaporavo climbed the steps, the last one to board, she was pleasant and professional. When she saw him, her eyes widened ever so slightly, which was enough. He glared into her pretty blue eyes, making her heart stop. He savored her fear a moment, then whispered to her that she ought to get off of the plane.

"Excuse me?" she asked. His eyes, when they cut sideways at the backs of the Hentzaus, as they picked their way down the aisle, said everything. She swallowed, nodded, and said *"Merci."*

Pushing past her, he waited for her to leave and start climbing down the steps before closing the door, thinking it would be nice to see the castle in France before going over to Morocco to free his family.

In Switzerland the next morning, well-rested, Guy hiked back to where he'd left his car, a wine red convertible Aston Martin, hidden inside a camouflage tent. Pressing a button on his phone, he made the tent fold itself up and pack itself into a small bundle, which he picked up and dropped into the trunk.

Hopping in, he put the top down and felt the cold wind in his hair as he drove into the mountains. He enjoyed the spectacular vistas that appeared now and then, when the grey of the rock parted; a deep wide valley, a rambling wood and the twinkle and glittering light of a sun-dappled river. The dancing gusts of color, of distant flowers tossed in the wind. A place where the stars were never dimmed by the pink aurora of city lights. And he dodged Alpine goats that came out of nowhere more times than he would have liked, until he came upon the remote castle perched atop a pine-covered mountain, looming forbiddingly in the crisp morning air, with its spires wreathed in wisps of cloud.

He pulled into the coach house beside it, parking alongside several other fabulous cars, grabbed his luggage, and went in the massive front door.

"Honey!" he called. "I'm home!"

Echoing from somewhere in the depths of that castle, a silvery voice called "Hello, Meester Booooooond!"

He came upon a breathtaking marble stairwell, dropped his luggage on a 19th century Persian rug on an immaculately polished parquet floor and dug his USB out of a pocket in one of the suitcases.

As he straightened, a beautiful woman appeared at the top and came bopping down the steps, her black ponytail bouncing behind her. Guy waited for her to get to the bottom and throw herself into his arms, and he held her to him and swung her around and around and around. The vaulted hall resounded with their laughter, and then their long kiss.

Ending with a smack, she smiled brightly into his eyes. "So…you have it?"

He made a contrite face.

"I *had* it."

"Ohhh, what happened?" she asked, her eyes wide with exaggerated concern.

"Well, it's a long story. It got pretty hairy there."

"I can imagine!" Then she playfully slapped him on the shoulder. "So hairy you couldn't answer your phone?"

"Yeah, well, I was tied up for a little while."

"Tell me all about it."

He put her down.

"I will over breakfast. If you don't mind, I'd like to get a shower. I had a very exciting day so I bet I smell a little…"

She wrinkled her nose at him. "No, darling, you don't smell a little. You smell a lot."

"It is the fragrance of action."

"And the um, file?"

He held up the flash drive and she squealed with delight, clapping her hands and snatching it from him.

"I can't wait!"

"I can't either."

"Go get yourself cleaned up and I'll have it ready when you come down."

They kissed again and she skipped out of the hall, while he picked up his suitcases again and climbed the stairs. At the landing was a waist-high ebony pedestal made to look like a Corinthian column, displaying the Hope Diamond. He did not even glance at it. At the top of the stairs, at the end of the hall, King Tutankhamun's sarcophagus stood as a sentry, the gold and lapis lazuli tying all the colors of the paintings in that hall together, just like Mrs. Fox said they would. He passed it as one would pass by a window.

In the kitchen, Sharon Dorothy Grace Fox plugged the USB into her laptop on a small round table, singing a wordless song of happiness, and waited for it to load. When the drive's only file appeared, she clicked on it and opened it with barely contained excitement.

Her face was bathed in white light as she scanned the pages of the document, scrolling down down down until it caught her eye—the words "Garlic Confit."

"Ah *ha!*"

She hunkered down to read it, her nose only a few inches from the screen.

"Wow, that's simple," she said to herself, and read aloud "Twenty-four cloves of garlic, peeled, and one cup of duck fat…*duck fat?* Oh, sweet Jesus, *that's* what it was!"

She got up and went to pull down a pan and turn on her stove, humming to herself.

When Guy came downstairs with his hair wet and some clean clothes on, Mrs. Fox was just finishing the eggs. The kitchen smelled divine, and she winked at him and told him to go set the table. He went to the hutch and took out the fine bone china, inlaid with gold fretwork, that was all they ever used. It had gone missing from Buckingham Palace a few years before, along with silverware of the most exquisite workmanship.

On the wall at the head of the table, behind Guy's chair, hung the Mona Lisa. Sharon had insisted they hang it there because it was her favorite painting, and she loved to look at her two favorite things while dining.

On an end table, stood an ornate chessboard with only two pieces, a queen and a pawn. Mrs. Fox had put it there as a piece of art, the significance of which Guy did not get.

He sat in his chair, a Louis Quinze bergère with foliate-carved gold beech wood and blue-beige upholstery that she had insisted he "rescue" from Versailles, along with one for her. She came out a moment later with two plates, putting one in front of him, saying *"Voila!"* She kissed him again, sweetly, and carried the other plate to her end of the table. He smiled down at the Croque Madame from Riposte, placed his napkin in his lap and waited for her to say Grace.

After saying Amen and getting ready to eat, she mentioned that it was sad he didn't get the painting after all. He nodded, hoping she wouldn't ask too many questions. He didn't like to lie to her, and didn't want to tell her he had given the painting back.

Especially since it would have *really* tied the sitting room together, what with the purple of the lady's kimono and all.

"Yunno," she said. "I read that the Russian imperial crown jewels are touring Europe, and will be in Brussels this month."

"Mm-hmm," he said.

Then, with their exquisite cutlery, he cut into the yolk and let it ooze all over the sandwich, mixing with the creamy sauce she had poured over it, sawed himself a bite, and speared it with his fork.

"And I was just thinking," she said, and gave him That Look.

"Mmm?" He lifted his fork eagerly.

"The queen's pearl and diamond tiara would go really well with that dress you bought me last week."

He froze with the morsel dripping sauce from the end of his fork, almost to his open mouth.

Looking at her, he sighed heavily.

Look for the Icarus trilogy, with

In Shining Armor

In Paperback

I

"We're designed to be hunters and we're in a society of shopping. There's nothing to kill anymore, there's nothing to fight, nothing to overcome, nothing to explore. In that societal emasculation this everyman is created."
—David Fincher

The second most horrible moment of Chandler Tuttle's life was the first time he played Russian Roulette at age seventeen. The second time wasn't as bad, a week later, but it was still unnerving. The thunder of his pulse pounding in his ears and the voice inside his head screaming "Do it! *Do* it, you little wimp!" culminating in a small heart attack at the sound of the dry, empty click of the hammer falling. He'd collapsed, gasping as all of his 'friends' laughed, ribbing each other with their elbows and pointing at him, then ruffling his hair as if he'd just lost his virginity and they were all proud of him. As his breathing returned to normal, he became aware of how much brighter all of the colors in the room seemed. How exquisitely formed were all of the objects it contained, from the perfectly-shaped bottles of booze on the shelves and the crystalline purity of the glasses. The sparkle of beautiful light reflecting on baroque ice cubes that settled and cracked in low-balls of sipping scotch. The tragic glamour of the Toulouse Lautrec-style burlesque poster on the wall. The kindly camaraderie of his friends sharing his moment of resurrection. That second most horrible moment of his life became, miraculously, the second most wonderful, and the two had become married in his mind from that moment on.

As the years wore on, he came to need that resurrection at certain points in his life. Sometimes it was after an opera, but always on the last night, of course. He would never think of leaving the show without its star if the hammer should fall on a live round. That would be more than just inconsiderate. As his friend

Richard would say, that would be "just the *height* of poor taste." No, he would wait until the last night, after all the fanfare and had died down and the champagne was gone and all the others had either paired off or passed out, and the great feeling of emptiness crept into his stomach.

Then he would slip away into the night and find a quiet place. He was also considerate of whichever poor sap would fall the burden of cleaning up after him. He never did it in his hotel room, where the scandal of it might ruin the fine establishment's reputation, and wallpaper. If he did it on a rooftop somewhere, he made sure to check the wind's direction. God forbid his brain (if, indeed, he had one) was blown away into the night to spatter someone's laundry drying on the line, or spot some couple's cheeks and ruin their first kiss.

That one night after singing the lead in the opera version of Dorian Gray, and getting that same ol' standing ovation as always, he had found a short wall to sit upon at the side of a river, spinning the cylinder blindly and putting the barrel of his snub-nosed Smith & Wesson .38 to the leeward side of his head, over his ear like his friends had been sure to advise him, instead of at his temple, and then he asked himself the same question he always asked.

"Are you ready?"

And he'd waited a moment, truly living in that moment and enjoying the crisp wind, if there was one, the twittering of night-birds, if there were any, and listening carefully for something that might stop him from doing it, like a beautiful young woman running up to stop him and say No! Don't do it! Toss that awful gun into the river and come have a coffee with me, and tell me your story and make me melt and fall in love with you, and we'll live happily ever after. Or words to that effect.

There was a distant chorus of car horns, and some people chattering excitedly somewhere. He adjusted his seating on the wall so that, if he should die that next instant, he would fall into the river and the people talking would not come running to find his body lying there in the darkness and scream, and have whatever happiness ruined. Got to be mindful of others, he reminded himself. It's very selfish to die making a spectacle of yourself.

He held his breath, closed his eyes, felt the rhythm of the world around him, felt at peace with it, let out his breath slowly and opened his eyes. And pulled the trigger.

Click!

And that time he didn't gasp in relief.

Somehow, on this, the seventh time, not blowing his own brains out was really no big deal. It was kind of, he hated to think it, a bit of a disappointment.

The eighth time was a pretty casual thing, too.

Kind of a non-event.

Ditto the next three, until he was really quite bored with it. He began to think he might be immortal, which would really suck, considering the circumstances.

The twelfth time, however, was a different story.

He'd sung a one-night show at the hotel Santo Domingo in Antigua Guatemala, back there in the lovely ruins of what had once been a monastery. They'd done the *Requiem* and, as usual, brought down the house. Champagne and kissy-kissy on the cheeks followed, everyone coming up to put their cheek near his and make sucking sounds with their lips pursed and then go off to squeal with delight at some other celebrity.

He slipped away early, that time, and wandered the quaint cobblestone streets, listening to the night-birds and the wind rustling the bougainvillea that tumbled down over the walls of one-storey buildings. The town was already asleep.

He didn't know where he ended up, just that he found a small ruin on a side street, an old tumbledown structure with lots of trees and bushes, and he decided it was good enough.

He climbed up, with some difficulty because the dirt was slippery and he didn't want to ruin his tux, just in case he survived again. He grabbed hold of branches and plants to steady himself, and fought his way to the top of a narrow slope that ran along the side of the ruin, and looked for a place to be comfortable.

This time, though, when he sat, checked the pistol's cylinder to look at the one bullet in there, and spun it, and took notice of the world and its sounds and smells, he heard someone. Being nosy, he looked for the source of the voices, and saw a small group of men moving stealthily along the narrow street. They didn't seem to be on a happy errand, so he shrunk himself, turtle-like, into his mental shell and made himself as invisible as he could. It is one thing to put a gun to your head and pull the trigger. It is quite another to be shot at by someone else. The men passed beneath him and continued on, and he, deciding not to mind his own business, followed them.

As quietly as he could, he moved up the slope to the edge of a building and hauled himself up onto the roof a few feet above his head. He scrambled quietly with his feet on the wall and made dirty skidmarks with his loafers before getting his elbows hooked onto the shingles.

Then, breath held, he tight-rope-walked across the apex as quietly as he could, all the while thinking that this was a really, really stupid thing to do, but it was better than dying or going back to his hotel room alone. Especially when room service had ended hours ago.

He slipped from one roof to another, which wasn't difficult since all of the buildings of every block were built right up against one another. Luckily, the bad guys were headed for the only two-storey house on the street, and it was the next one. It had a lighted window on the second floor, and he crept up to it with as much stealth as his loafers allowed.

He couldn't see how the bad guys were getting into the front door, but they were, and not with the attitude of welcome visitors. In the room of the lighted window was a white man who looked a lot like Chandler, in that he was dressed well with clean-cut good looks and a boyish face. While Chandler's brown hair was swept forward in a Caesar cut, his had that forward-and-up look that was just coming into style. He was pulling strips from a roll of duct tape and sticking them by their ends to the cellophane wrapped around what looked like ...oh dear, were those pound bags of weed?

Chandler gaped for a moment, and then started to laugh silently to himself, thinking Of all the windows to creep up on!

The young man's head snapped toward the door, and he whipped his supple body into a crouch, his hand going instinctively for a gun on his hip that wasn't there. His eyes darted all around the room looking for where he must have placed it while his mind was on other things, but it was too late. The men entered the room with someone else, a young Guatemalan woman in guipil and corte, the traditional woven top and long skirt that the Indigenous wear. She was held between the two biggest of the six men, all of them dark and menacing. Three of the other four held pistols in their hands, and the fourth came into the room with an evil smirk on his cruel thin mouth. They all looked at the young man with rapist eyes, and the unarmed one spoke in Spanish, moving toward the bundles of marijuana and laying a hand on the corner one, stroking it lightly.

Chandler understood a smattering of Spanish (and French and German and Italian) but couldn't make out what the leader was saying because the window was closed. He was suddenly thankful that the light was on inside with no streetlights to betray his face on the other side of the glass. The window was a mirror to everyone inside.

I should go, he thought. I really, really should.

Poor guy inside, though, and poor housekeeper or whoever the woman was. But that's why you don't get into the drug trade, he thought.

He watched the leader advancing slowly on the white man while he spoke, his bearing unmistakably threatening, until he stopped with their noses maybe two inches apart.

He said something else, turning his head and pursing his lips, jerking his chin at the housekeeper, and looked back into the young man's eyes, smiling wickedly.

And the young man's head tilted back slightly and snapped forward, breaking the dark man's nose and bloodying his face. Chandler and the other men in the room jumped, shocked, unbelieving, as the young man ducked and jabbed his fist into the man's solar plexus, rose and grabbed a handful of his hair, stepping backwards to make room and jerk him around as a human shield. One hand slipped underneath the Guatemalan's armpit and came back around to grab his Adam's apple, his fingertips digging into the bristly throat.

"Run that by me again?" he snapped in English.

The bad guys shouted and pointed their weapons at his head, but he said "I wouldn't!" like "I wouldn't if I were you," and when they made to hit their hostage, he dug his fingers in deeper and made that sharp *At!* noise that one shouts at a dog when it's about to do something wrong.

The leader was trying to struggle, but the young man's fingers just dug in deeper and deeper, making the man's dark face go hot and red.

Chandler couldn't believe it. What *guts* this kid had! In one moment he turned the tables and went from being another statistic to being…well, probably another statistic anyway, but one who would at least take the leader with him, and Chandler liked that. He liked it enough to step in. He inched his way back from the window and pulled the snub-nosed .38 out of his tux jacket's side pocket thinking Glass doesn't shatter outwards, does it? Not when it's shot from outside, right?

He leveled the .38 at the foremost gunman, aimed square at his chest, then reconsidered and aimed at the face, just in case the guy was wearing a bullet-proof vest, and was planning on squeezing the trigger until it went off when *bang!* the window exploded, and the gunman fell backwards into his colleagues with a bloody ruin of a face.

Jesus, Chandler thought. That one was for me.

If this hadn't happened, my number would've been up.

The young man was staring over his shoulder at him, his eyes wide, and Chandler felt he should say something. Something clever, but couldn't think of anything. He just pointed his now-empty (but nobody *else* knew that) gun at the henchmen and said reassuringly "And this is what they call Deus Ex Machina."

The young man gasped a startled laugh and turned back to face the bad guys, who were spitting and wiping blood and brain matter and shards of bone out of their eyes, looking like they were completely at a loss.

"Drop 'em!" the young man shouted, then remembered himself and said *"Armas al suelo y manos arriba!"*

They hesitated, looking at their leader, who gurgled. They tried to back out of the room and Chandler jabbed the gun at them and screamed, repeating what the white man said. The goons let the housekeeper go, and she swatted their guns out of their hands in sudden fury and kicked one of them over to her master, the young man who summarily tore out his hostage's throat and shoved him forward to stagger and fall while he snatched up the gun at his feet.

The young man fired rapidly, blowing the others backward through the door, the housekeeper jumping and crying out in fear.

Chandler's fist shook, the gun smoking in his hand.

The young man looked at him over his shoulder again and said "You're not going to shoot me with that thing, are you Mr. Deus Ex Machina?"

Chandler coughed and said "Um, it's empty now."

The guy laughed. "You're kidding!"

"Nope. I only had one. Long story."

"Oh my God, I can't breathe. Where the hell did you *come* from?"

He held out a hand to help Chandler climb down through the window, and the opera singer kicked out jagged shards of glass before accepting.

"I'll explain later. I suppose we ought to leave."

"Well, yeah, I imagine we do. What's your name?"

"Tuttle. Chandler Tuttle."

"Like Bond, James Bond."

"Ha! Yeah, I guess so. And you?"

"People call me Rabbit," the young man said.

Acknowledgements

The fictitious history of the Family Hentzau, as well as the "alternate history" of world events were based on a timeline of the Rothschild family by Andrew Carrington Hitchcock, and is used with his permission. The author is eternally grateful. That timeline was based on information from the following sources:

Proofs of a Conspiracy Against All the Religions and Governments of Europe Carried on in the Secret Meetings of Freemasons, Illuminati and Reading Societies - John Robison - 1798

The Life of Napoleon - Sir Walter Scott - 1827

Coningsby - Benjamin Disraeli - 1844

The Communist Manifesto - Karl Marx, Friedrich Engels, Martin Malia - 1848

Morals and Dogma of the Ancient and Accepted Scottish Rite of Freemasonry - Albert Pike - 1872

The Rothschilds, Financial Rulers of Nations - John Reeves 1887

The Jews and Modern Capitalism - Werner Sombart - 1911

Great Britain, The Jews, and Palestine - Samuel Landman - 1936

Pawns In The Game - William Guy Carr - 1937

Inside The Gestapo - Hansjurgen Koehler - 1940

Barriers Down - Kent Cooper - 1942

The Mind Of Adolf Hitler - Walter Langer - 1943

The Empire Of The City - E. C. Knuth - 1946

The Jewish State - Theodor Herzl - 1946

The Curious History of the Six-Pointed Star - G. Scholem - 1949

Secrets Of The Federal Reserve - Eustace Mullins - 1952

Tales Of The British Aristocracy - L. G. Pine - 1957

Red Fog Over America - William Guy Carr - 1958

A Jewish Defector Warns America (Spoken Word Recording) -
Benjamin H. Freedman - 1961

The Rothschilds - Frederic Morton - 1962

The Illuminati and the Council on Foreign Relations (Spoken
Word Recording) - Myron Fagan - 1967

Ben-Gurion: The Armed Prophet - Michael Bar-Zohar - 1967

The Hidden Tyranny - Benjamin Freedman - 1971

None Dare Call It Conspiracy - Gary Allen - 1972

The Gulag Archipelago, Vol. 2, Parts 3 and 4 - Aleksandr Solzhenitsyn - First English translation published 1975.

Wall Street And The Rise Of Hitler - Anthony C. Sutton - 1976

The Rosenthal Document - Walter White, Jr. - 1978

Two Rothschilds And The Land Of Israel - Simon Schama - 1978

The Six Pointed Star - Dr O. J. Graham - 1984

The Last Days In America - Bob Fraley - 1984

Who Owns The TV Networks - Eustace Mullins - 1985

The Samson Option: Israel's Nuclear Arsenal and American Foreign Policy - Seymour M. Hersh - 1991

A History of the Jews in America - Howard M. Sachar - 1992

Deliberate Deceptions: Facing the Facts About the U.S. Israeli Relationship - Paul Findley - 1993

Descent Into Slavery - Des Griffin - 1994

Bloodlines Of The Illuminati - Fritz Springmeier - 1995

Jewish History, Jewish Religion - Israel Shahak - 1994

Satan Speaks - Anton Szandor LaVey - 1998

The Elite Serial Killers of Lincoln, JFK, RFK & MLK - Robert Gaylon Ross - 2001

Never Again? The Threat Of The New Anti-Semitism - Abraham H. Foxman - 2004

The Elite Don't Dare Let Us Tell The People - Robert Gaylon Ross - 2004

Many of the details regarding the CIA are from: The Brothers – Stephen Kinzer- 2013

The country Ruritania, the city of Zenda, and the name Rupert of Hentzau are from *The Prisoner of Zenda,* an adventure novel by Anthony Hope, published in 1894. The villainous Rupert of Hentzau from the first novel gave his name to the sequel published in 1898. The books were extremely popular and inspired the new genre of "Ruritanian romance."

Before Zogthar the Great was allowed to visit the Earth, he was forced to sign a waiver promising he would only observe the people of this planet, not interfere. He has since reneged on that promise, blending in with Earthlings and going under the name Alexander Ferrar, and has founded a restaurant, art gallery, and exotic ice cream company in La Antigua, Guatemala. He is also the author of ten other books, and the painter of realistic and surrealistic art that hangs in private collections all over the world.

His autobiography *Memoirs of a Swine* is in stores now.